What's True, Darling

M.A.C. Farrant

Previous Short Fiction by M.A.C. Farrant

Sick Pigeon (Thistledown Press, 1991)
Raw Material (Arsenal Pulp Press, 1993)
Altered Statements (Arsenal Pulp Press, 1995)
Word of Mouth (Thistledown Press, 1996)

What's True, Darling

M.A.C. Farrant

Copyright © 1997 by M.A.C. Farrant.

This book is a work of fiction. Names, characters, places and incidents are products of the author's imagination or are used fictitiously. Any resemblance to actual events, locales or persons, living or dead, is entirely coincidental.

No part of this publication may be reproduced, stored in a retrieval system or transmitted in any form or by any means without prior written permission from the publisher, or, in case of photocopying or other reprographic copying, a licence from CANCOPY (Canadian Copyright Licensing Agency), 6 Adelaide Street East, Suite 900, Toronto, Ontario, M5C 1H6.

Polestar Book Publishers acknowledges the ongoing support of The Canada Council, the British Columbia Ministry of Small Business, Tourism and Culture, and the Department of Canadian Heritage.

Some of the fictions in this collection first appeared in the following magazines: "Family Baggage" and "All Chickens Are Sucks" in *Geist*; "Jigsaw" in *The Malahat Review*; "The Playground Supervisor" in *Matrix*; "Dorothy Parker's Dog" in *Contemporary Verse 2*; "Diana Ross in Wax" was produced, in slightly different form, as a chapbook in the Spring of 1997 by *fingerprinting inkoperating*, Toronto. With thanks to damian lopes.

Cover design by Val Speidel
Cover photograph: "Cabaret Dancers" from the Gordon Anthony
    Collection, 1973 © Hulton Getty/Tony Stone Images
Author photograph by Terry Farrant
Printed and bound in Canada

CANADIAN CATALOGUING IN PUBLICATION DATA
Farrant, M.A.C. (Marion Alice Coburn)
    What's true, darling
    ISBN 1-896095-28-3
    I. Title.
PS8561.A76W52 1997   C813'.54   C97-910816-0
PR9199.3.F355W52 1997

LIBRARY OF CONGRESS CARD CATALOG NUMBER: 97-80430

POLESTAR BOOK PUBLISHERS
P.O. Box 5238, Station B
Victoria, British Columbia
Canada
V8R 6N4
http://mypage.direct.ca/p/polestar/

In the United States:
POLESTAR BOOK PUBLISHERS
P.O. Box 468
Custer, WA
USA   98240-0468

5 4 3 2 1

For Pauline Holdstock
with love

And for Pops, Rodney, Martin,
Henny, King, and especially Terry,
Daddy o'mine

Special thanks to the following people for their support and generosity: Carolyn Swayze; Alma Lee; Michelle Benjamin, Emiko Morita and Lynn Henry at Polestar Press; Joan Henriksen; and to Jo-Anne and Norman Dobell.

The support of the Cultural Services Branch, B.C. Ministry of Small Business, Tourism and Culture is gratefully acknowledged.

Starring Lotta Hitchmanova

Starring Lotta Hitchmanova ... 11
Dorothy Parker's Dog ... 19
The Delightful Sayings of Ho Min ... 27
Diana Ross in Wax ... 35
Closing Time at Barbie's Boutique ... 53
Jigsaw ... 59
All Chickens are Sucks ... 63
Blague Mountain ... 69
Virginia was the Hardest ... 71
The Globe ... 73

Family Baggage

Hallowe'en So Far Away ... 79
The Playground Supervisor ... 83
Tales from Wit's End ... 87
A Short Manual on the
  Care and Cultivation of Boring Relatives ... 107
Little Zerotta ... 119
Tic-Tac-Doe ... 129
Weird Pets ... 147
Built for Pleasure ... 157
The Party ... 167
Family Baggage ... 175

"Tragedy and limelight may be
everyone's special event but what's true, darling,
is that it's all wonderful, every last bit of it."
— "Sacred Tales, vol. 2"
from *Hiding Place of the Comediennes*

Starring Lotta Hitchmanova

Starring Lotta Hitchmanova

IT SEEMS TO BE WORKING. Our bid to lionize Lotta Hitchmanova is gaining ground.

I'd sent a press kit to the Powell River City Council, telling them my entourage would be arriving in two months' time and to please prepare the presidential suite at the best hotel. "It's an important cross-country tour," I wrote in my covering letter. "Lotta Hitchmanova, that wonderfully kind Communist in the quasi-military suit, will be reviving her famous USC tour."

Official response was warm. The Mayor, as it turned out, was a great admirer of Lotta Hitchmanova. He faxed a return message. "I can't help it, but I get sentimental when I think of her," he wrote. "Every October during my youth the local paper ran her picture, a grainy black-and-white head shot — Lotta Hitchmanova in her peaked cap and military jacket with the spray of medals across her breast — and an announcement about where she'd be giving her talk, collecting clothing and medical supplies for the orphans. We always went, Mom and me, to the Unitarian Church Hall. It was during the Cold War. But I thought Lotta Hitchmanova was dead. I'm so glad to hear..." Etc. etc.

We felt enobled by the Mayor's message and proceeded with our plan.

On the agreed date, we pulled up at the Town Hall in our twin cars — brown 1981 Toyota Celicas. The dignitaries waiting for us on the steps didn't bat an eye; they believed it right and proper for a goodwill ambassador to be travelling in a vehicle one step removed from the junk yard — an appropriate, and dare I say brilliant, display of humility on our part.

There were just the two of us in the entourage: my assistant Buzz, and me as Lotta Hitchmanova. But the officials didn't flinch at our small numbers, either. Proving my point once again that the world is in need of goodness. In dire need of goodness, hungry for it; people are prepared, these days, to embrace goodness at the drop of a peaked cap.

I was pleased, therefore, with the reception. A red carpet was unfurled and a child dressed in a costume from the nineteenth century stumbled forward to present a bouquet of flowers. Next, a suitably long receiving line: Women wearing hats from the fifties curtsied, men in grey flannels clicked their heels and nodded. A good beginning, I thought, and a tribute to the way things can be carried off if you know how — if you have the right bearing.

And I know about bearing. It's all in the coming and going. I've studied the entrances and exits of celebrities: It's all in the way you get in or out of a car and walk through a crowd. The way you smile (not too warmly) at the People, how you stop for a ten-second chat with the wheelchair bound or the visibly ill.

It's in the way you glance. Glancing is a skill I've particularly studied: the glancing over the left shoulder while going in and out of public buildings. It has to be done at the right moment. And there must be a hint of shyness in the glance, as well — of breathlessness, although you are in complete control. The glance occurs just as you enter the building, leaving the throng on the street, and it must convey regret to the adoring crowd, regret that you cannot linger with them. The message embodied in the glance must be: If only there was enough time...if only we could chat over one or two bottles of *Concha y Toro*. Crowds are happy with such a glance; it's called the "human touch." It makes your celebrity, your elevation, tolerable. It's what I do so well — well enough to manage this first-ever Lotta Hitchmanova impersonation. Buzz and I want nothing less than celebrity status for Lotta Hitchmanova, the world's newest goodwill ambassador; we believe it's our public duty to put her image forward.

We were shown into the presidential suite and everything was in place: the banks of calla lilies by the window, the pair of king-sized beds, the huge box of chocolates, the complimentary vibrator (Ah, life at the top!).

Dinner before my talk was as expected: the *de rigeur* salmon steak with stuffed pimentos; the English custard with sauce *Bellemerde*. And Buzz, sombre as a funeral director in his black suit, sitting beside me at the head table. Relieved that he doesn't have to fuss about protocol like he usually does during VIP impersonations — staying in the kitchen and tasting each mouthful of food before I can eat ("I'm not into regurgitation!") or playing my personal assistant and carrying the tray of lace handkerchiefs, in case one should be required for the VIP tear or the VIP snot or the VIP drool.

We've said it time and again: It's amazing the way people will ignore everything when faced with celebrity; they just fall down and lose control before people they've decided are superior beings. They become, in a sense, blind. Even when he is playing my assistant and wearing a pink linen suit and modest hat, Buzz's beard has been ignored. And then there's the mauling issue — Buzz's biggest complaint. The crowd may not be able to touch the VIP, but they can certainly maul the assistant. Which is what they frequently do. In fact, expect to do. As soon as the famous last glance has been cast and the celebrity is safely inside the building, the crowd rushes for Buzz. To touch the one who waits on the Important Person. For a souvenir handkerchief, particularly if it's been used. For a souvenir piece of Buzz's clothing or hair. During our last Madonna impersonation, he was quite shredded and bruised.

"I can really get behind Lotta Hitchmanova," Buzz said later in our suite. He was opening a bottle Bordeaux and eyeing the complimentary vibrator in anticipation of a VIP workout. "It's like a holiday. It *is* a holiday: free food, free hotel. And everyone so nice and well-behaved; I didn't get scratched even once. For the first time out, Lotta Hitchmanova was a success, even if the only donations we got were old clothes and some canned goods."

I agreed. There was definitely a heightened interest in Lotta Hitchmanova — a general sympathy and readiness on people's part to accept Lotta Hitchmanova as the world's newest Wonderful Human Being. And I was pleased with my peformance during the dinner: first, my dance at the gala ball, where I'd again displayed the "human touch" by briefly kicking up my heels during a geriatric rendition of "The Peppermint Twist." And then, wearing Lotta Hitchmanova's trademark peaked cap, and with a display of studied shyness, I gave my speech. Using a strong Eastern European accent, I said: "Suffer unto you thee leedle children...Minny, minny orphans go hongry...Tousands of ennycint veecteems die in the vorld ebbery day...We haf to do our share." And so on. Next morning we thought it best to slip away early. We feared overstaying our welcome and breaking the Lotta Hitchmanova spell.

So we abandoned the new routine until next time and, congratulating ourselves on a successful event, did a hasty Michael Jackson — face mask, black hat, ten-year-old boy — and slipped out before dawn.

Two hours later and in another town, Buzz pulled into a parkade. I followed in my matching Celica. He said he was hungry. So Michael Jackson and his young friend strolled hand-in-hand down the busy main street. Within moments, a crowd was following us.

"Breakfast time," Buzz announced, and a restaurant door flung open. We were escorted to the best table, where the *maitre d'* presented us with brocade-covered menus. "Order what you like," Buzz said. "It's on the house, of course."

I tossed a glance over my left shoulder, towards the crowd peering at us through the restaurant windows. Several flashbulbs popped. A waiter refilled our juice glasses and, smiling ruefully, Buzz and I toasted the crowd. A cheer went up. The cheer was so prolonged that the head waiter hurried outside to ask everyone to please keep it down. "After all," he admonished, "the celebrities are entitled to some privacy, aren't they?"

Abashed, the crowd agreed. Content now to press their noses and fingertips against the restaurant windows, staring and staring.

Dorothy Parker's Dog

WHEN I CAME HOME FROM THE HOSPITAL I discovered my friends had redecorated my room at the Algonquin. They'd draped the bed and writing desk, the couch and chairs in black cloth and they'd hung things from the ceiling — framed pictures of condemned murderers, carving knives dangling from strings. There was even a length of rope draped artfully across my bed. And they'd placed an assortment of step ladders around the desk in case I felt like climbing. The effect was bleak but charming. Ironic decor.

They thought I'd be pleased. I was pleased, after a fashion. By the gesture of the thing. Who were these friends? I don't know, the usual blur of revved up people. Somebody this, somebody that. What does it matter who they were? Background music, bit players, atmosphere for the macabre piece.

Whoever they were, they got the idea from me, from what I'd done while in hospital. You see, I'd attached a small orchid corsage to each of my bandaged wrists. Yes I did. Nasty of me, I know, but it made me laugh at the time, gave me a kind of grim satisfaction. Perhaps I'd ordered the corsages from a florist myself, perhaps I'd sent one of my friends to fetch them. I don't remember. But the orchids were pale mauve in colour and hard as wax. And I had this delicious thought: I will be a sarcophagus, flowers sprouting from my near-bloodless form. Cleopatra. That's who I had in mind. I'll be Cleopatra lying in my hospital bed, pale and calm, my corsaged wrists lying still above the covers.

I received my friends like this, visiting hours being the same time as cocktail hours, four to six. When they saw me they screamed with laughter. *Oh, our Dotty's so wicked!* And opened the champagne bottles and the bottles of Scotch. We drank to my cleverness. Thirty or forty friends partying in my hospital room. All the twinkling New York gnats were there — writers, editors, the round table drunks, all the bright young things. I got fairly lit mixing the Scotch with the sleeping tablets; after that I was gone for days.

How many times did I attempt suicide? Every time a party ended. Every time I put pen to paper.

Doesn't that sound grand? But it's a full-fledged lie. Which, of course, I excelled at. Lies and more lies. Here she lies and I don't mean Cleopatra. Oh the wordy girl! Suicide or murder; I was adept at both, though it was by pure accident, this trickery with words.

For some reason I was called upon by the New York circle to train as their magician. And the first thing I learned was running with my nose to the ground. Oh, I could sniff out the idiots! *You can lead a whore to culture but you can't make her think.* You see, I was a natural; spite and sarcasm flowed easily. This is where my fame lay — in the caustic line, harsh enough to wither any reputation! People were delighted, craved the personal insult. The more they laughed, the nastier I got until a party wasn't a party until I was there.

But there were things I loved more than words: Scotch and dogs top the list. I've always preferred a dog to a man and I've had a string of both. I can remember all of my dogs' names — but the names of the men! Not a one.

Robinson was my favourite dog, a Dachshund; he went everywhere with me. Our day began at five with cocktails in my room at the Algonquin. Now you're not to believe the reports that Robinson shit on the rug. People assumed this because I never rose before noon and where would the poor dog do his business? Where indeed? On the pages of the *New York Times*, where else? Spread about the floor, awaiting Robinson's annointment. Since waking up was not the best part of my day, jittery and bitchy as I often was, inspecting Robinson's deposits gave me a small pleasure, like a throw of the dice: Robinson the fortune teller. I was always delighted to see whose writing he'd chosen to shit upon — some upstart critic venturing onto my turf, some pathetic reviewer attempting a Parker line (everyone knew I was Constant Reader at the *New Yorker*).

So Robinson was my researcher. And the smell? There was no smell. Darling, that's the beauty of hotel life: maids. Each day at four they'd come in to clean, air the place out. And then at five cocktails began. Twenty or thirty people would stream in bearing gifts — I loved receiving gifts — usually bottles of Scotch or little things to eat or a toy for Robinson. Everyone drinking and laughing, everyone so gay, and then all of us piling into taxis for a night at the clubs, Robinson tucked beneath my arm like an enormous sausage.

At the clubs he'd curl himself beneath the table. A group of us drinking and there Robinson would be fast asleep. (Something I'd always wished men would do, sleep at my feet.) But he'd start awake and follow me whenever I moved; he'd even follow me to the Ladies and wait outside the stall.

WHAT'S TRUE, DARLING

Such devotion! I'd order waiters to bring him bowls of water or chopped meat, and many of the young men hanging about would be called upon to take him outside to do his business in the street. And they daren't refuse me. After all, I had them by the short hairs: Refusal to do their duty by Robinson meant banishment from my terrible, envied circle. And not one of them would risk that!

A wonderful dog, Robinson. Cecil Beaton begged for months to take my picture and I consented only if Robinson could be in the picture as well. I told Cecil: You mustn't photograph me close-up, I detest that sort of inspection — you must take my picture from a distance, as if I'm glimpsed from across a room at a crowded party or a hotel lobby, as if people were saying, "Ah, there goes Mrs. Parker. You know who Mrs. Parker is, don't you? Why, she's..." The darling of the New York art world, I might have added — the *enfant terrible* at the heart of the literary scene.

The picture Cecil finally settled on as his creation has me seated formally, a side shot facing left. I'm dressed for the outdoors in a hat and a long coat with a fur collar, and I'm holding a fur muff; you only see half of my face, which was fine with me — I've never been terribly excited by my own face, too tiny and dark for my liking. In this picture Robinson is placed on the ground and facing me so that his body is in profile as well; his head is cocked, his muscular body taut, expectant.

My beloved Robinson; I never let him out of my sight. He even escorted me when I spoke to the Dream Come True Club. This was during the height of my fame — people couldn't get enough of me. It was a very swank club in the upper Eighties; several hundred members turned out. After a fine meal of Scotch and more Scotch I rose from my perch at the head table and gave the speech.

I told the audience how I'd really wanted to be a famous fire-eater, wearing a black sequinned gown and a red feathered hat, the flame in my torch threatening to immolate me there and then. I told them that this writing of words is pale by comparison — there's no hoopla, no costumes, no real danger. Any fire we writers consume is of our own making — the stuff of sound and air — and if our words are not hot enough, do not set hearts and minds aflame, if what we hurl into the world doesn't catch fire...

The applause was generous, the audience pleased. They liked how I had settled for second best, this writing of stories and verse. Afterwards, several of them asked for my recipe for writing success and I wrote it down on small index cards: three parts bullshit, one part spit.

Shortly after, I told this story at a party of Edna's. Oh, I was lit. The party was to celebrate something or other; we were never short of things to celebrate. Edna's new book of poems perhaps. We were all gathered in the garden because Edna was showing us her outdoor writing table, a perfectly boring wood table set beneath the trees. Who the hell cares about her writing table? I mentioned as much to a man standing beside me. Darling, I told him, you wouldn't believe where I write my things — in bed, on the john, in the back seats of taxis. Oh, I do believe I'll conduct a tour of my john the next chance I get, I told him, and he laughed.

Anyway, people went on and on about Edna's table, several of the crowd slobbering, practically licking the cursed thing when this odious woman, one of those overly dressed society matrons, bosom extending from neck to knee, spoke up, declaring to Edna: So this is where you do it! This is where you construct your famous poems. Reaching up to the overhead sky with those skilful hands and grabbing fistfuls of dappled light. Stirring this light into your poems. So that's how it's done; this is why your poems glow.

You want glow, I shouted, I'll bet you've never seen a fire-eater. And I flicked my lighter, arched my neck and opened my mouth. The crowd gasped, jumped back, then fled. Edna grabbing her book of poems lest they fall prey to a stray spark. Everyone gathering inside the house to sip champagne and pop cool cucumber sandwiches into their admiring mouths. (My mouth has never admired anything.)

Leaving me to perform alone in the garden with Robinson as my only audience. It was a wonderful performance. Not a flame wasted, not a delicate nose hair singed. A performance executed smoothly and in the grand eccentric condition. I am, after all, an idiot savant for beauty.

There we were in the garden. My grandest performance. With Robinson watching, panting and blinking his applause.

The Delightful Sayings of Ho Min

HO MIN, THE ANCIENT MASTER, SAYS: "I was once held upside-down over a cliff by an unruly feudal lord and while in this position wrote twelve verses. And, oh, the exquisite upside-down pain!"

We first saw Ho Min at the National Gallery — a tiny, oriental man covered in rags. We were on our way to see the Munch paintings — wonderful, enormous paintings that filled entire walls.

Rodney said, "Imagine that! Allowing a beggar inside the National Gallery!"

A friend later told us about Ho Min and then we remembered the beautifully carved eleventh-century beggar's bowl he had been holding and were intrigued. At first it was the *idea* of him that compelled: Ho Min hovering around the edges of our official creativity, grinning in his tolerant, wise, oriental way. Our colourful world-sized canvasses, our important booming utterances. And Ho Min grinning at the way we bite our knuckles in despair, trying so hard to impress!

Ho Min says: "Avoid pathways because they have a right side and a left side, a beginning and an ending. You must always be in the middle of nowhere."

Before Ho Min: the usual story. Rodney and I car-bound on the freeway, the daily ninety-minute commute. Dragging ourselves into our mortgaged house at day's end, collapsing on the chesterfield with martinis. Our boring sex lives. Our lack of interest in food. The vague medical complaints: aches, irritability, fatigue.

Rats on the wheel and all that.

But since Ho Min: *Context*! A great lasso framing our exhausted lives.

WHAT'S TRUE, DARLING

Ho Min spends much of his time tending the giant babies. A tiny figure wandering amongst the rows of giant cribs. The crib legs reaching to shoulder level where the crib platforms begin; several Ho Mins could fit between the slats of the crib bars. The babies squeaking and gurgling. Smiling. Drooling.

We ask him: "What is it with the giant babies?"

Ho Min says: "Diapers, wheat-free cereal, educational toys, the usual things."

Ho Min's preferred methods of locomotion: skipping, hopping, dancing, ambling, crawling. Sometimes, draped over the back of a disciple. If he's in a madcap mood: tricycle, roller coaster, jet.

He refuses to ride in a car: "Too in-between."

Ho Min says, "The perfect form of travel is the community park swing. It's got everything: height, speed, forward and backward motion and yet it goes nowhere. What a supreme invention! What a metaphor!"

"Metaphor?" we humbly ask.

Ho Min says, "Smoke and mirrors. Razzmatazz."

Ho Min says: "Mentally, we need a halfway house. Some place between here and there. Know of any good bordellos?"

Sometimes Ho Min makes us angry. For example, when he says: "It's not with the eyes that we see, it's with the mind. Better to be blind than to have the shelf life of a mayfly — that brief flapping against the window pane, that long, twitchy death..."

We throw the book at him then, our great work-in-progress, *The Delightful Sayings of Ho Min*. "Not even slightly delightful!" we scream.

Ho Min, that rogue, scampering for cover beneath the branches of a lovely acacia tree. Calling out to us: "Ha, ha, ha, ha!"

When Ho Min takes a break from tending the giant babies, he dons his plastic beauty-queen wig and gold lamé gown and wanders the city streets looking for love.

Commenting upon our indignation, Ho Min says: "Sometimes there is nothing to do but primp and screw."

We worry about Ho Min's absorption with sex. We believe it unfitting for a sage to be so...involved. Is there nothing else on his mind?

"Mind? What's mind?" Ho Min demands.

"Well," we stumble, "higher consciousness? Past lives? Eternal wisdom? The seven levels of this and that?"

WHAT'S TRUE, DARLING

"Fools!" Ho Min screams. "There is only nothing and everything. And some of it is covered in icing and some is covered in shit."

Ho Min has a serious thing about cars — beyond the business of being an in-between form of travel. He says that every time he rides in a car it races backwards, out of control and the brakes won't work, the steering goes awry.

Ho Min says: "Cars scare me."

We are startled by such a pedestrian anxiety; surely a wise man would be above such fears. "What is death" we remind him, "but a journey to the inevitable?"

Ho Min sighs. He takes his Ming dynasty brush — still wet from his latest, inexplicable poem — and draws it across his lips, indicating: My lips are sealed.

A line of black paint stretching across Ho Min's grinning face.

Ah, the paradoxes of the master!

Ho Min and the giant babies: "My current temple," he says, his face crinkling with delight. "They're over-blooming with life. Look at their massive fists and thighs, bellies, cheeks. Each baby weighing one hundred, one-twenty-five. They gurgle and grow, have moments of clear blossoming. They smack with delight at rays of sunshine. Sleep the sleep of oblivion. Sleep with their mouths open. Bubbles forming at the rims of their wet lips. There's something to be understood here."

"But what?" we ask.

"The way we're always looking in the mirror. Explaining the changes. Of ourselves, our times. The difference between what's observed and what finds itself occurring."

"Huh?" we say.

"If I had a two-by-four," Ho Min sings to the tune of the Dylan song.

Ho Min is prone to tantrums.

Rodney has been called upon to cart the master on his back to Zellers department store. But Rodney has back problems and there's the exhaust from the many cars. There's the staring factor. "I don't mind in the privacy of our own home," Rodney pouts. "Or in the woods. Or along the sea cliff. Or even to the corner store. But I'll be damned if I'm going to cart him along Highway 151. And have everyone gawking."

I fear for Rodney's...something...but can't put my finger on it.

Ho Min is livid. He twists Rodney's ear. "Vermin!" he shouts. "Eternal piss-off!"

But Rodney won't budge. "Even if you hold your breath," he tells Ho Min, "I won't do it."

Ho Min considers for several moments then laughs. "You very good disciple," he finally says, slapping Rodney on the back, "call me a horse and buggy."

Ho Min's sleeping place: the Hall of Giant Babies. He sleeps on his side, legs bent, naked. In his sleep he's smiling, while overhead the babies coo like mammoth pigeons.

Rodney and I watch the sleeping Ho Min. "He really *knows* something," we whisper to each other. "He's got *answers*." If only we could break Ho Min's code...But like all sages, he scatters his clues, keeping us puzzled.

We are two of a handful of disciples scurrying behind Ho Min, recording his sayings. Then, at our yearly convention, we compare notes, adding to the Great Work (*The Delightful Sayings...*) which is our testament to Ho Min's sagehood.

There's Larry, who first introduced us to Ho Min; John and Jimmy on the Rideau Canal, who are designing a Ho Min fountain (something with medical tubing and glass beads); Petra, an exotic dancer who doubles as Ho Min's personal trainer; and old Mrs. Simmonds, our next door neighbour who took to him immediately. "He's so cute and skinny," she told us later. "Like a rag doll. You just want to squeeze and squeeze him."

Sometimes Ho Min attends our Ho Min Conventions. Usually he doesn't: the master off doing inexplicable masterly things, like tending the giant babies; the disciples liking the word "inexplicable." We've taken it as our Ho Min masthead, courtesy of the OED: "That which cannot be explained or accounted for."

The latest entry in our Ho Min book:
It is said that Ho Min works in his studio seated in an eighteenth-century chair with a back shaped like a scholar's hat. It is also said that his desk is a delicately carved haunghuali desk and that to pen his poems he uses an ivory-handled Ming dynasty brush.
At such times we imagine Ho Min dressed in a pristine white shirt, poems drifting to the page like single wet leaves.

At the Ho Min Convention: seven disciples sitting cross-legged on the floor, eating take-out Chinese. Pondering the many sayings of Ho Min.
What can they possibly mean?

Diana Ross in Wax

The Early Years

MRS. BREWSTER SAYS...

    That girl was the wildest, always getting away from me; she may have been small but she was wily. Many times I'd see her on the street riding some boy's shoulders, pretending she didn't know her own mother; I suppose she liked the view from up there. But I was always afraid for her, that she'd fall off and damage her head. She kept her hair short in those days — didn't wear the wigs she wears now — and so didn't have much protection if she hit the pavement.

The other thing was men's pyjamas. Always wearing Daddy's or her brother's pyjamas. "Why you gotta look like Sweet Pea?" I'd scold. But she'd pay me no mind. We were poor but we weren't *that* poor; she could have had her own pyjamas — special tiny ones, I would have sewed them myself — but she wouldn't have it. Had to be men's pyjamas, and flannel ones at that, and so long in the legs they dragged behind her when she walked or else dangled down the back of whichever boy she was riding. She'd wear those pyjamas day and night, going out in them like you and me would wear skirts or pants. It got so no one paid her much attention. "Oh that's just little Darlana Brewster wearing her pyjamas," people would say, causing her old Mama pain.

But Darlana remembers things differently. Always griping about how she started out, recounting the slimy climb to what she figures is a better life. Telling anyone who'll listen. Lies, I'm bound; we never treated her so rough.

DARLANA BREWSTER TALKS ABOUT HER TROUBLED BEGINNING...

It's about my ladder; I was always losing it. I'd go to the cupboard at the back of the garage to get it and it'd be gone. Who was stealing my ladder? I needed that ladder; there were places I was climbing to and that ladder gave me independence. It was a good ladder made of lightweight aluminium, shiny. I kept it well maintained; it never gave me any trouble. Except when it went missing. "Mother," I'd holler, "where's my ladder?"

"Oh," she'd likely say, "Mr. Miles down the road has got it, he needed to get on his roof and since you weren't using it…" Or some such thing. And then I'd have to track it down. How could I get anywhere without my ladder?

Another thing that griped me: birthday presents. How many times did I have to say, "High heels, I want high heeled shoes." Was the world deaf? Year after year it's high heels I'm wanting. But what did I get? Tiny pearl drop earrings. Pearl drop earrings! Cleverly hidden in a high heel shoe box. Every birthday I'd be climbing on the table, tearing at the wrapping paper. And every birthday it was the same: The family gathered around me laughing, splitting their guts.

Lack. That's what I had. Lack of regard. Lack of a decent sized body. So it was a natural hunger; I wanted to be bigger.

THE FAMILY DOCTOR COMMENTS…

Yes, Darlana Brewster is a midget. Not an ugly, misshapen dwarf but a midget, a perfectly formed miniature human being, thirty-five inches tall. She stopped growing at four years of age (didn't respond to growth hormones) but otherwise has developed normally. She has tiny hands and feet, tiny teeth, tiny, tiny ears, a tiny mouth, the teensiest brown eyes…

GENERAL TOM THUMB OFFERS ADVICE...

I tell this to all my midget colleagues: Find your niche, capitalize on your times. Look at me. I could have wasted away in Bridgeport, Connecticut, an object of ridicule and shame, but my mother had foresight; she sold me to P.T. Barnum to exhibit at his American Museum in New York city. Barnum changed my name from Charles Stratton to Tom Thumb after the midget who rode a mouse in the King Arthur legend and was killed by a spider. He dressed me in an exact replica of a cavalry uniform and said, "Tom, you're so cute and brave in your uniform you should command a midget army!" And that's how I got the "General" before my name; it was pure showmanship. I was billed as the Smallest Miniature Man in the World.

And the crowds flocked. Three thousand people came to my grand debut, where I performed a "wrestling match" with the celebrated giants Monsieur Bihin and Colonel Goshen and then recited Yankee Doodle Dandee. I was an overnight sensation. Very quickly I became rich, owned houses, yachts, race horses, kept the company of beautiful and demanding women. Queen Victoria presented me with a miniature carriage only five feet long; I was received by all the kings and queens of Europe.

By the 1850s I was the biggest star in the western hemisphere.

WHAT'S TRUE, DARLING

THE RECORDING GURU REMEMBERS...

She parked herself outside my office door, this cute little girl — said she was seventeen years old — and no taller than three feet, couldn't have weighed fifty pounds. But big on determination she was, persistent. Day after day she'd be there waiting to see me, dressed in a tiny pleated skirt and matching jacket, a teased wig, and on top of that, a pill box hat. She had a plastic bag full of men's pyjamas with her and this aluminium ladder parked on the floor beside her. But it was the outfit she wore to my office, that's what impressed. She had the look of the times down pat, a perfect replica but miniature like an ornament, like something you'd put on a shelf. And somehow she made the bigger girls look like clowns, like they were taking up space, getting in the way. "What you want, child?" I'd say. And she'd give me this big smile — a huge smile, that smile was the biggest thing about her — and she'd say, "Why, to be a big star, you dolt."

It didn't take me long to soften. I started carrying her around on my shoulders. "You can throw away that ladder," I told her, "you won't need *that* no more." We were some pair.

MISS HONEY RECOLLECTS THE FINISHING SCHOOL DAYS...

Right from the start the boss had the idea to take that girl, that sassy bit of nothing, and make her into something big. It was a sight to see the two of them, the girl riding the big man's shoulders. Why, they'd walk the streets like that, go to fancy restaurants! Didn't care if people laughed at them, didn't care one bit. The boss told us, his staff, "You're gonna treat Darlana Brewster like she's the biggest thing since sliced bread." Oh my, he loved that little girl.

So I started a school to clean them up, all the boys and girls that were going to be his singers and make him rich. Many of them still fresh from the ghetto, didn't have no idea how to act.

First off, I changed Darlana's name. "Darlana Brewster's no name for a star," I told her. "You need something high class, dignified." And came up with the name Diana Ross. Then I told her, "You want to be a star? Then you gotta learn to shine. And there's no way on earth you're gonna shine carting around them men's pyjamas." So we throwed them out.

Oh, they laughed at first, these kids, because of what I had them do. They didn't take it serious, all this prancing about, walking with books on their heads. What I did: worked at making them look pleasant. So big night-clubs would hire them. I told those boys and girls: "It's not where you come from, it's where you're going." And I wanted them going places. I taught them how to handle a mike so the mike doesn't handle you. Taught them to sing with their eyes open. Another thing, the most important: we got their teeth fixed. Then I taught them how to smile, a wide, prideful smile. Diana Ross' smile was the widest. I showed her how to smile without showing her gums, not an easy thing to do. Showed her how to smile while singing. She was an eager pupil, learned fast, got so she could smile eating a hamburger, smile in her sleep.

It was the boss' idea to make her lead singer of a girl trio, put her with a pair of big lumpy girls so she'd stand out. "Like sticking a flower with a bunch of leaves" is how he put it.

I was worried at first, because she was so small, but then I went to work. Twelve-inch wigs, platform shoes, stilts beneath long flashy gowns. The false rump and breasts were Diana's idea to give her body shape. The heavy black eyelashes were her idea too. She stole the look from that white skeleton Twiggy.

THE DANCING TEACHER REVEALS...

The boss come to me said, "Benny we got to teach these kids how to dance. Not that old stomping dance them poor people do in the south but something polished, more uptown, a kind of crossover dance that'll sweeten Ed Sullivan into having us on his show, that'll cause middle-class folk to stampede into record stores and buy our records."

And that's just what I did. I took Diana Ross and her backup singers and rehearsed them for three months. I told Diana, "You gotta move so the fellas really notice what you're putting down." Not an easy thing for her to do, propped up on stilts or platform shoes the way she was, and wearing those sky scraper wigs. But she caught on, she wanted stardom bad. She'd fling her arms about and twist her shoulders in time to the music but keeping the focus off the part of her body that wasn't moving, her legs. She never pranced about the stage — she couldn't — but we managed to make her seem dignified standing in one place. The long dresses and the spotlight helped. After the show was over and the curtain come down, stage hands would carry her to her dressing room. Then she'd be arranged on a chaise lounge and surrounded with giant baskets of flowers so she could hold court to well wishers and the press. The boss liked to stand to one side during these times watching her, grinning with pride.

So all that rehearsing paid off. The trio debuted at the Copa to rave reviews. Pretty soon they had a string of hits — the boss kept the writing team busy day and night — and we were on our way: Vegas, the Sullivan show, the New York clubs. Didn't matter that her voice was whiny and she sang through her nose. We turned her singing style into an advantage. And we made her elegant. That was our brilliance. Wrapping that puny kid with the lousy voice in satin and furs and selling her to Whitey.

WHAT'S TRUE, DARLING

THE SECRETARY RECALLS "MISS-ROSS-TO-YOU"...

About her being a midget, that's another thing. And I wouldn't say "midget." We never used that word around the boss — it'd get you fired. We learned to never refer to her size. And then what the boss had us do was call her "Miss Ross." Not Diana, using her first name like we did with the other singers, but "Miss Ross," that's what it had to be. And Diana started demanding it, too. "It's Miss Ross to you," she'd say superior-like to anyone who addressed her wrong — make-up people, stage hands, the other singers, us secretaries in the boss' office, people in the press. So behind her back that's what we started calling her: Miss-Ross-To-You.

Diana, Herself

BABY BABY, OOH, BABY BABY...

Fifteen hundred lovers couldn't take the place of warm nights in the recording studio with you. I always meant to. I always had our union in mind. I said, "Keep me riding on your shoulders and we'll be hearing symphonies all the way to the bank!" Before long you'd singled me out, asked me to cut a country album, sing Gershwin, ditch the trio and launch a solo career. All of which I eagerly did. What I was interested in: your promotional savvy. That and having yachts and power and class and public reverence. Your love, too. I didn't mind that. Your big hands stroking my tiny, tiny...

DRESSING FOR SUCCESS...

...A gold lamé and chiffon gown with dolman sleeves...A black velvet dress punctuated with pearl and gold braid at the neckline and with a trumpet-shaped shirt flaring out at the ankles...A long-sleeved black sequinned gown, the sleeves embellished with gold rick rack...Several red sequinned gowns...A pale pink taffeta sheath with tiny white pearls encrusted diagonally on the bodice and skirt...A silver satin pantsuit with matching sequinned vest and black ascot...A white sequinned Bob Mackie gown with matching cape...A dragon-sequinned yellow satin

WHAT'S TRUE, DARLING

kimono...A powder-blue lynx coat...A full-length mauve one-shoulder gown with matching marabou feather muff...A green-and-white dyed foxtail coat and matching celebrity sunglasses...

DREAMING ABOUT THE LADDER...

Vacuuming the living room rug in my ball gown, a blue taffeta formal. The exact shade: blue-eyed devil blue. And the phone rings, it's Mother shouting: "What are you going to do about these dead leaves on the roof?"

"Dead leaves? You think I'm going to climb your roof in my party dress? Wrong," I say. "I'm going dancing." And swirl around the sudden dance floor with my partner Mr. White. He's wearing a formal tux and though he prefers long wet English youths, he says I'll do. He's got one hand dangling over my shoulder and the other clutches my legs at his waist.

The dance floor is crowded. Any combination of dancer is possible, like a classified ad: men with men, women with women, old with young...even animals — a horse, its mane braided with red ribbons, prances by with three girls on its back, a dog on its hind legs dances with a woman in a black sequinned gown. Even Jack the Giant Killer is dancing; he's collected a pack of rival girl singers and is leading them in a conga line to his beanstalk, that great leafy ladder to the clouds...

Excerpts from the Unauthorized Biography

HER UNAUTHORIZED LEGEND...

"Three girls from the ghetto become a popular singing act. The man who owns the record company becomes the lover of the lead singer and makes her the focus of the act, elevating her to stardom. The lead singer eventually leaves the group for a solo career and then stars in several motion pictures — all produced by her lover. Only one of the movies does well. Along the way, the lead singer garners wealth, power and public reverence (but only one yacht), and a great deal of bad feeling from those she tramples on in her climb to stardom. She eventually discards her lover, who by no means suffers, having become a multimillionaire with many coveted possessions to his credit including a dude ranch and a string of coin-operated laundries..."

HER UNAUTHORIZED MEMOIRS...

"I can still see that Christmas evening when after the concert I found the whole family drinking whiskey. Mother, tipsier than the others, danced her great Indian dance. And off in the corner my brother Jackson struggled on the floor with his ungovernable sexuality. 'Down, boy,' he was saying in alarm. 'I do believe I'll have to build you a cage in the basement!'

"This was the evening my oldest brother Redmond tried

to hurl himself out the living room window. Mother interrupted her dance to grab him by the foot and just in time. Someone called 911 and Jackson was encouraged from his corner to sit on Redmond until help arrived.

"The 911 team was there in minutes and wrapped Redmond in clear plastic. 'Oh, goody,' Redmond shrieked, 'smother me in plastic, put me in a giant zip-lock baggie and throw me in the freezer.' The 911 worker said, 'No way, you're going to the Karate school, you'll be perfect for the students to practise on — one deranged man ripe for flipping.'

"At midnight the rest of us sang 'Stop! In the Name of Love!' and then I fled to my own cosy mansion. Comfort is needed not only from the snow flakes which whisper at the window, but from my house staff of fifteen, my showpiece bedroom with walls of white brocade, my white satin dressing gown trimmed with marabou feathers, and my devoted toy poodle Lenore."

HER GREATEST FEARS...
1. Impoverishment:

Darlana and Mrs. Brewster panhandling outside the liquor store, sitting side-by-side in a cardboard box, a saucer before them and a sign that reads: *Diana Ross Fan Club: Donations Welcome.*

2. Ridicule from fans:

Diana Ross is a midget! We were so shocked. Even wearing her foot-high black wig, she's a midget. Even with the stilts and sequinned gown — still a midget. And her solo performance at the New Year's Ball. Shy and embarrassed she was. Grateful, even. When we'd expected glittering, commanding. Dare we say 'glowing.' And so some of us were suspicious. We'd paid good money and there was a midget on stage pretending to be Diana Ross. We wanted "Baby, Baby, Where Has Our Love Gone?" but what she sang was the French national anthem and "Good Night Irene." Good Night Irene! A supreme irritation, if we can be allowed the pun.

HER RATING SYSTEM FOR AUDIENCES...
 1. Warm
 2. Most fair
 3. Partial crowd
 4. Scattered applause
 5. Heavy disdain
 6. Force one humiliation
 7. Protection needed

HER THOUGHTS ON THE NEW MUSIC...

I don't understand these younger singers. They're like method actors, so insistent on being themselves in their ratty clothes, with their hoarse voices. They're without style or training, without boundaries. And so many of them crowding me off the stage. A flood of urchins, unwashed, howling their songs of despair. Whatever happened to love, hope, glamour?

What I think: There's no profit in being yourself.

Diana Ross In Wax

The order was for an eight-foot-tall model, larger than usual but not a difficult job.

First, working from publicity posters, we made a clay mould of the head and then took a plaster mould from that. We filled this plaster mould with a combination of vinyl resins and plasticizers, tinting the mixture Honey Brown #37. At this stage, the head was without hair, eyes or features.

Next we sewed in the head hair strand by strand, over half a million hairs. We opted for this method over using a wig because of the close scrutiny paying customers would give the model. Hand-sewn human hair is more natural looking, more authentic.

The eyes weren't as time consuming as the hair. We used medical glass eyes and inserted them from within the mould. Much effort was taken to set the eyes at the right focus; we had the model looking into the distance, as if towards the back of a theatre. The "sparkle" in the eyes was achieved using diamond dust.

The teeth were a special order. Naturally, we had the model smiling and our requirements were that no gums be showing. Our dental people had to make a special set of teeth because the teeth in normal usage are too small. Point five millimetres were therefore added to each tooth to achieve the proper proportion. When the teeth were inserted, the hair was styled and our make-up artists went to work.

We used our in-house hand model for the hands, dipping them in plaster then filling the mould with the plastic resin. Fortunately, we could use synthetic nails that could be painted red.

Once the head and the hands were done it was quick work to complete the figure. We used a standard six-foot fibreglass body and dressed it in a long gown made of red sequins. With the hair teased and wearing high heels, the figure reached approximately eight feet and three inches.

We then positioned the model on one of our stage sets, the head tilted slightly as if in song. We made sure the eyes were open. We made sure the facial expression was one of rapture. A tiny speaker lodged behind the teeth played a constant medley of the star's hits.

Closing Time At Barbie's Boutique

"THE PROBLEM," BARBIE SAID TO SKIPPER, "is the ones with fat arms and purple-white skin. They buy something sleeveless and want to wear it home. Then you have to reach up to their fetid armpits and cut the tag. It can knock you over."

"I hate the ones without underpants," said Skipper. "Yesterday a woman trying on a jump-suit wanted help with the buttons and right there in front of me was her bush. No way was I going near that thing."

"What did you do?" asked Barbie.

"Nothing," said Skipper. "They all think you're their mother: love them, love their warts, don't care how they look. I just hung the jump-suit back on the rack and hoped some dummy doesn't get a social disease from trying it on. I'm just thankful I don't have pubic hair."

"Amen to that," said Barbie.

"I wish, though," said Skipper, "that I didn't feel so miserable. Sometimes being human seems almost attractive."

"Bite your perfect lips," said Barbie. "What you need is a change. Why don't you do something with those braids?"

"Yes, I could definitely do with a change," said Skipper.

"You should get out more," said Barbie. "Have a few laughs. Too bad I'm saving seal pups in the Arctic next weekend."

"Couldn't I come along?"

"Not this time," said Barbie. "I promised Ken. He's taking pictures of me for my Christmas Sticker Book."

"Oh," said Skipper. "Tough tit, them's the breaks."

"Cheer up," said Barbie. "Think about the seventeen midgets in here last week wanting car coats."

"That was funny," said Skipper. "Or the time the hunchback wanted an evening gown."

"Yes, that was a laugh," said Barbie. "Very funny. Then there was that bus load of women all celebrating their one-hundredth birthdays. Came in just to look around. Erotic pawing of lingerie."

"I liked the male nurses," said Skipper.

"They all slobbered," said Barbie. "I saw them slobbering. Drooling, lusting beasts."

"I could do with one of those," said Skipper. "A drooling, lusting beast would just about fit the bill."

"Never heard from Brad again? Where'd he get to?"

"A younger model," said Skipper. "Traded me in for a younger model. One of those new flexible jobs that bends at the knees. A stick with legs. Why do these things happen? What's the matter with perpetual twelve?"

"Nothing's the matter with perpetual twelve," said Barbie. "At least you're not close to mature. Like that antique in here this morning. Did you see her fingernails? Enough dirt in there to start a rooftop herb garden. Wanted polyester."

"Figures," said Skipper.

"Even so," said Barbie, "I have my principles. I won't sell something that looks bad on a customer."

"Unless," said Skipper.

"Unless," said Barbie, "they're beyond hope. And many are beyond hope. Most are beyond hope."

"The flowered silk on the fatties," said Skipper.

"The black and purple bikinis on the stringy broads looking like they're on they're last bag of dog food," said Barbie.

"How do you do it?" said Skipper. "How do you keep Ken?"

"Well," said Barbie, "I'm always light and gay and full of fun. Plus I'm not bad looking."

"You're a knockout," said Skipper. "You're a beautiful American doll."

"Make the most with what you've got," said Barbie. "Work on your personality."

"If only I had your hair, your perfect nipple-less breasts," said Skipper.

"Well, you *are* supposed to be only twelve," said Barbie.

"I want your longer legs," said Skipper. "Your Crystal Barbie Gown."

"Always look on the bright side," said Barbie. "Learn to be a good sport. In a pinch, dreamboats like Ken just love plucky little girls who are good sports."

"I'll bet," said Skipper. "Like the one in here on Tuesday? Ooze of good sport?"

"Not that much good sport," said Barbie. "Horse teeth, saddle thighs. It makes you wonder. People, they're quite revolting. The one in here on Ground Hog Day. A walking cadaver."

"Sequinned suit, no bum?"

"The very one," said Barbie. "Imagine being all tarted up at eighty! Bird bones dressed as nouvelle cuisine. Imagine having a life and having it just about over."

"It boggles the acrylic hair," said Skipper.

"Thank Mattel we're spared all that," said Barbie. "The

worst that can happen to us is competition from newer, more supple models. But they'll never have the prestige we have. We were here first; we're quality."

"You really think so?" said Skipper.

"Of course," said Barbie. "We're number one. We've been around a long time and we're still as firm as ever. You've still got your original lip paint! And consider this: we lose a leg, no problem, a new one can always be found — whole businesses are devoted to manufacturing parts for us. And you can't say that about the human models; it's the green garbage bags for them before long."

"The worst that can happen to us," said Barbie, "is being left too long in the sun — the slow melt of our features. Or being tossed from a car window by an unpleasant child. Or being left to soak too long in the bathtub and having black mould growing around our neck-, arm-, and leg-holes. And even if some child cuts off all our hair, it can be replaced in any colour we want. But it's best not to dwell on negative things. That's Barbie's Motto. And when you think of it, most of us are cherished and you can't say that about humans. And we have the best, most fashionable wardrobes, too. Some of us even have our own boutiques! And swimming pools! And southern mansions!"

"I fear the feminists," said Skipper. "The leather pants and crew cut brigade. They'd be happy if we didn't exist. They'd like nothing better than to melt us down for dildoes."

"Nonsense," said Barbie. "They probably played with us when they were little. Everyone's had a Barbie."

"I don't like the sound of that," said Skipper.

"Are you still fretting about Brad?" said Barbie. "Look on the bright side. At least you don't have a hairless head. Like the one in here on Halloween."

"What did it want?" said Skipper. "Trick or treat?"

"Combat boots," said Barbie.

"Ha, ha," said Skipper. "I think I'm feeling better."

"Good," said Barbie. "If you stay close to your friend Barbie, you'll concentrate on the carefree days of youth, your days will be filled with adventures and you'll always be smiling. Now don't you think it's better to be a doll?"

"Yes. Yes I do," said Skipper.

"I'm glad to hear it," said Barbie. "Now help me unpack this carton. It has my new Swiss Chalet inside and I can't wait to try on my ski fashions. And if you promise to keep smiling and keep that pretty little head of yours empty, I just might find something in here for you to try on, too."

Jigsaw

OH THAT LEONARD COHEN. He turns up when you'd least expect him. Dinnertime, for example, when we're sitting down to our meagre meal, our Gregorian Chant meal, it being several lifetimes before payday. I was just dishing up the beans to those of us humbly assembled and turned to my left and there he was sitting next to Henny calm as you please.

I'm very fond of beans, Leonard Cohen said, looking searchingly into my eyes, lingering he was in my eyes, we were having what you might call a moment of hesitation across a sea of beans. And I said yes, I love beans too, they being high on my list, right up there at the top of my list of poverty food, and I love a man who loves beans. And Henny, a man who's loved without hesitation, said, yes, good old beans, we all enjoy a satisfying meal of beans, but not any beans, not canned beans or boiled beans or fried or sautéed beans but *raw beans*, these being the most economical way to imbibe bean nutrition and we're everything for nutrition at this table, yes everything, because sometimes there's little else to think of.

Leonard Cohen smiled, I believe it was wisely, and slowly nodded his head, his dark-haired head with its sculpted Roman nose and its cheeks flushed with a scandalous hint of pink. I was about to ask him his thoughts on the culture of beans, his views on this subject, but first I said, surely there's poetry in beans. And he smiled again into my brown beanie eyes and said, yes, dear lady, there's poetry in beans, in figs, in cashew nuts, you name it, we're rolling in poetry, it's just a matter of being Aldous Huxley and opening the doors, peeling the eyeballs, baring the skin and this is often everything. In fact, he continued, I'm sure there's more skin in the world than asphalt and if all the skin was laid flat, laid end to end, we'd have a new membrane with which to cover the earth, replacing ozone, replacing our dank and fumey skies. Yes, I said, baring our skin is a necessary concept because that's what the children are doing this very minute, razor blading their emotions with the help of Aldous Huxley and blotter acid. Can't you hear them howling? I asked, a cluster of children at the back of the house howling their heads off that the sky is falling, the sky is falling, not liking their eyeballs flayed, not liking it at all?

Leonard waved his hand. It means nothing, he said, nothing at all. But I was impelled by the urgent something and had to leave Leonard Cohen to eat his beans alone as we, the rest of us at the table, but principally Henny and me, rushed to quell the children's hysteria. Hysteria of the usual kind, to be sure, but raw hysteria, that being the best way to imbibe new emotion, new vision, which is what the children were doing. By the time I'd handed out the blankets, re-read the old stories and settled the children, I found Leonard sitting outside on a collapsible deck chair jotting in a notebook, serene Buddha that he most certainly is. (But a wee bit disinclined for all that, I thought, to get his pinkies wet, his elbows muddied.)

Henny then said, as we rested in the sun at Leonard's feet, Henny said, well Leonard Cohen, since we're all liberals here, can you tell me your views on nothingness? But didn't get to expand on his theme because Leonard got mad, got huffy and said, I never defend a thing I've researched. And with this utterance got up and strode out of the yard.

So there's another piece of the puzzle gone missing and if this keeps up we won't have a puzzle at all, just a series of holes and spaces. You start out life with the puzzle intact like an enormous jigsaw and then one by one the pieces drop out or go missing; every time you ask a question, shake your head and admit you just don't know, a piece of the puzzle goes missing. Every time you approach a Leonard or a Don or a Julio or a Grace and ask them to tell you why and how, it's tits up for another piece. If all the holes and missing spaces were laid end to end, I said to Henny, if all the unanswered questions were gathered into a giant bouquet...And Henny sighed, gazing about the empty yard. Nobody here but us chickens, he said. And we left it at that, returning to the supper table and our meal of beans. Shaking our heads. Nodding our heads. Pecking at our plates of beans.

All Chickens Are Sucks:
Notes from the Litshow

---

1. A MAN ASKS IF HE CAN PRAY before I begin a reading, kneeling in the café and asking for God's protection. This was in a dream. The same dream in which my reading was sabotaged by a young Jehovah's Witness poet who flung my books into a bank of blackberry vines.

2. I give a reading on a B.C. ferry. Over a hundred Japanese tourists are in attendance. All of them are asleep

except for one, who is manning a video camera. It occurs to me that I often see Japanese tourists sleeping en route — heads slumped against bus windows, bodies leaning into each other in airport lounges. But there's always one or two taking pictures. Perhaps they draw straws to pick who will stay awake and do the filming. Perhaps they gather, later on at home, on their day off from the corporation, to view these slides and videos. All of them amazed and delighted by what they slept through. In this way having a kind of second vacation.

3. A literary agent writes to say he's interested in representing my work. He wants to tell me about his clients, most of whom, he says, are professionals in one field or another. "There are medical doctors," he writes, "Ph.Ds, an Indian author who used to be a movie star, a lady veterinarian pilot who has spread her wings into adult mysteries, an eighty-five-year-young medical missionary with a wooden prosthesis (leg lost to gas gangrene in her early thirties) who has worked for over fifty years as a nurse in the remote regions of Northern India. There's a…"

4. An organizer who has a German accent gives me details about an upcoming reading: "You will catch the three-thirty ferry. Dinner is served promptly at five-thirty. The reading begins at seven-thirty. You will read for forty-five minutes.

Then there will be a lengthy coffee break after which you will read for another forty-five minutes. You will sleep on my couch. If you bring your husband, he will sleep on the floor."

5. Driving to the town in southern Saskatchewan which has become famous as the home of junior hockey coach-pedophiles, the reading organizer tells me that there is one word I cannot say during my reading. "It's the four letter word beginning with 'c' and ending with 't,'" he says. "They just cannot abide that word." I ask him if the four letter word beginning with "f" and ending with "k" is all right. Also the seven letter word beginning in "a" and ending in "e" which is used for rear end. "Are these words okay?" I wonder. These words, the organizer assures me, are fine: "There's no problem with them. But they'll walk out if you use the 'c' word."

6. After seeing me on a cable interview a woman acquaintance telephones. "You did very well," she tells me, "but I noticed that you used a lot of 'ums' and 'ahs.' I can help you with that. I'd like to invite you, as my guest, to the next meeting of Toastmasters International. It's at the Silver Threads. You go in the front door. But don't turn right. That's Bingo. Turn left." I instantly decide I love my "ums" and "ahs." I'll keep them. It's what saves me from sounding like I'm in sales.

7. After a reading I sleep in the home of a woman who is enamoured of angels. Small, glittery angel forms appear on tables, floors, countertops. They're everywhere, like air freshener. There are also angel sayings placed here and there. On the sewing machine: *Every blade of grass has its own angel.* On the typewriter: *If everyone only listened to their angel.* On the bathroom mirror: *Make angel wings ten times.*

A large poster in the bedroom where I sleep is titled "How To Be An Artist." The poster lists several things I can do to become one: invite someone dangerous to tea; make friends with freedom; swing high on a swingset in moonlight; give money away; believe in magic; laugh a lot; take moon baths; draw on walls; giggle with children; play with stuffed toys; build a fort with blankets; hug trees.

The poster is colourful; there's an angel blowing a golden trumpet in each corner and the how-to instructions are printed against a large rainbow. A Care Bears ambiance hovers in the room. In the morning I flee. As I'm getting in my car, the woman calls gaily from the front steps, "You never know when you'll be touched by an angel!"

8. A book reviewer creates a prize. It's made out of an empty cereal box. He calls it the "Wet Salami." I am one of seven winners. It's possible I dreamt this. The winners are required to perform a musical number on stage; all of us

wear identical blonde wigs. One of the winners plays the piano, the rest attempt a chorus line. I then step forward to deliver a speech of thanks. Looking back at the other winners I notice that they are all idiots, drooling sub-normals happy to be fêted. Each of us is holding a wet salami. One of the idiots is eating hers.

9. I give a reading before twenty-four empty black chairs. The reading goes well. There is nothing dreamlike about this occurrence. The reading goes well because I've given up all hope of an audience ever arriving; it's become clear that the twenty-four chairs have become my audience. I therefore conjure up significance: There is something exquisite about the way this double semicircle of chairs has hurled me into the moment, something…er, wonderful…about the way I've crashed into where I am. Which, on this rain lashed Wednesday evening in mid-December, is exactly nowhere — or as Donald Barthelme would say: nowhere — the exact centre.

10. At the last minute, my publisher changes the title of my new book to *All Chickens Are Sucks* and puts me in charge of promotion. This may or may not be a dream. I take my duties seriously. At the book launch I wear a chicken outfit and sing in a chicken squawk the theme song from *Saturday Night Fever*: "Stayin' Alive." Then I read ex-

cerpts from the book. Every so often I let out a terrible chicken screech. For my finale I settle myself on the floor, grunt several times and lay an egg. Everyone rushes for the book table. The publisher immediately begins a second printing.

Blague Mountain

IN DESPERATION, THEN, SOME OF US disfigured ourselves in the name of Art. Becoming the Slasher Poets, razor-blading haikus onto our backs and thighs. Others of our kind found success as Tattooed Children's Writers, covering our bodies with illustrations from our books — a special privilege for children, the live performance, curious hands tracing the figures displayed on our colourful backs and arms. Some women poets shaved their heads — not the whole head just the top — in a simulation of male-pattern baldness and then combed thin strands over their shiny domes. And founded a School, a Movement, calling it Blague Mountain — a raucous gathering of semi-bald, drunken, flannel-shirt wearing, cigar smoking, women poets whose Anti-Minimalist Manifesto included celebrating the adjective, the formerly reviled and dependent adjective — and some writers were allowed to join the movement and some were not. Other writers turned to history, plundering the look of another time, and so costuming became important — ball gowns, uplift bras; there was a flurry of romance writers exposing their breasts on national TV. Amongst male fiction writers, cardinal's robes appeared at book launches. And nun's habits, Gilbert & Sullivan pirates, three-piece suits from the jugular of the corporate world. All for media interest. All for the coveted author profile, the scant review. The work is supposed to speak for itself, one novelist complained, but it takes too long to say what it has to say. This from the woman who had a hair implant on her chin and upper lip, thus becoming the Bearded Lady Novelist, renowned on three continents...

Virginia Was the Hardest

I WRENCHED THE SHOTGUN AWAY FROM ERNEST. Talked the razor blades out of Dorothy's hands. Was walking by when Diane hurled herself from the twelfth-storey window. She fell on me but lived to take more tortured pictures.

Sylvia required some cash outlay: I hired an army of contractors to seal every oven door in the vicinity of her English cottage. All Janice required was conversation: Look, I told her, I'll make sure everyone loves you; you can end your romance with pills and booze.

Vincent needed persuading but in the end was grateful for my diagnosis; somehow he found it calming to know his visions had a name. When Edgar barricaded himself inside his chamber, I slipped a petition under the chamber door — twenty thousand names begging him to hold on, give the world another try.

Soon after, I bought a warehouse. Filled it with crates of whiskey, cartons full of pills. With plastic hoses, ropes, guns, knives, syringes. Locking everything away. And still they tried to leave us.

Virginia was the hardest. I waited at the seaside for years. When the time came, I was there to haul her into the late twentieth century. It's because of her I've had to eradicate the sea; it's a desert now where the hopeless wander.

The Globe

THE GLOBE WAS KEPT IN THE SCIENCE LAB. A small world it was and alive. A female world, we were told, one that was worried about dying.

It was hard to believe that this blue-and-green papier mâché ball was alive and some of the students doubted it — some teaching trick to get us interested in Earth Science 11. But the teacher told us: "Oh yes, she's certainly alive. We've done many experiments and discovered we can communicate with her using written notes. She can't see but she can hear and so we read our notes aloud to her."

"What do you tell her?" Harder, I think it was, called from the back of the room. "That she's got awesome curves? That her blue skin drives you crazy with desire?" Laughs all around.

But some of us were intrigued and wanted to pick up the globe and have a look. Mr. Dyck, the teacher said, "Certainly not. I told you, she's afraid of dying. What if you dropped her? What if you tore her covering?"

"Oh, we won't, we won't," we told him. "We'll be really careful." We'd been trained since kindergarten with the "hands on" approach and wouldn't be denied.

So we lined up. "One at a time," Mr. Dyck said nervously. "And keep your voices calm and your movements slow; she doesn't respond well to agitation."

Each of us took a turn handling the globe. One student put it to her ear and said, "I can hear a tiny heart beating!" Another said, "Oh, the blue part's so crinkly it's scratching my hand."

Harder, ahead of me, was next in line. "What a load of crap," he said, grabbing the globe which was the exact size of a basketball. He tossed it to his friend Lawrence, who started dribbling with it.

Mr. Dyck was there in a flash, calling us a bunch of morons and telling us to sit down. He put the globe on his desk and it made me feel sorry. Because right in the middle of Mr. Dyck's speech about responsibility the globe tried to commit suicide by rolling off the desk onto the floor.

Mr. Dyck caught it just in time, hissing at us: "See what you've done? It'll take months to undo your stupidity."

Then he was hurriedly writing a note, bending towards the globe and whispering: "Don't worry, my precious, I'll look after you. I'll make certain no more harm comes your way."

Family Baggage

Hallowe'en So Far Away

HOME AND THE UNDRESSING BEGINS. Suits, dresses, overalls, masks. The workday world becoming a pile of clothing and props heaped at the living room door. It's evening now and we can relax, sip cocktails, become who we really are.

Some of us are twelve feet tall! And the day has been a torture of smallness, folded as we are into three-piece suits. Our bodies cramped, our limbs bonsai'd into awkward shapes. What a relief to finally stretch; two full strides and we're in the kitchen pouring wine.

The hunchback's relieved, as well. He's spent the day as a cashier at Volume Discount wearing a harness so he'll look like everyone else. But his hump is aching, his back sore from standing straight. Now he removes the binding that conceals his form, and the glass eye that hides his empty socket. Removes the platform shoe from his left leg, allowing his game leg to drag free.

There are others, too. A witch removes her teeth and blonde wig, settling onto the sofa, gin and tonic in hand. What a pleasure to leave the library behind, allow her voice its wondrous range; cackling and shrieking, she pulls bent fingers through dry, black hair. And executive secretaries, ward room nurses: from their backs unfold fairy wings as delicate as origami sculptures; now they can draw their curtains, hover about the light fixtures without gossip or scorn.

Home, and even used-car salesmen are transformed, rushing to bathroom sinks and erasing workday faces to find relief: vampire pallor and bloody lips exposed. And teachers! Peeling off their teacher masks, clown faces erupt; sore red noses are massaged into bulbous shapes, enormous feet spring forth from Cinderella shoes. But some of us *are* Cinderella, hiding our prettiness inside stiff power suits. Our days are spent as businesswomen, entrepreneurs; we've been talking out the sides of our mouths, shouting down the opposition. Now we can don our rags, wash our floors in peace, dreaming of rescue — the Hallowe'en Ball. Only in the sanctity of our homes, this revealing; our one public night so far away.

Only at home. Where the Kings and Queens amongst us can tear off drab workday clothes. We've spent the day disguised as bureaucrats, faking humility. Now we can unleash our secret majesty, anoint one another with the tissue-covered crowns we hide in our dresser drawers. We're lighting the candles, filling the goblets, discussing over dinner our plans for the realm. How much to spend on the dependents? The children, the dog, the cleaning lady who acts like a serf? How much for the banquet, the RRSPs, the winter vacation, the ermine robe? And which bloody daytime war will next receive our royal assent?

The Playground Supervisor

SPRING AT LAST, A TIME OF LUST AND CHATTER. Over there, several small boys wear their mother's brassieres atop flimsy T-shirts. It's Brassiere Season and the trading is fierce. What's prized? Large cups, the larger the better. Black ones, white ones. All colours! And in lace, cotton, spandex. But it's the bland beige ones with the enormous rubber cups that are most desired. These brassieres have the strength of sling shots and are often used that way — armies of boys hurling missiles of dirt at each other during their fierce, roaming wars.

But the favourite use for brassieres is to fill them with sand and stones, and tie them to their chests with hope and imagination. Then the boys play "Knockers," strutting about the playground cockle-doodle-doing, knocking one another over with their bulky breasts. They're fond of nursing brassieres, as well, loving the flaps. Another game: flap tag — chasing and spraying each other with the brassiere's sandy contents.

During Brassiere Season you can always tell the mothers of small boys; they go about their business unhinged — their ponderous melon breasts a special delight to the grocer, the gas jockey, the manager at the bank. But it's a sad season for boys with small-breasted mothers. Everyone laughs at them! Their meagre brassieres stick on their chests like postage stamps; you couldn't knock over a fly with such puniness. Faring worse are the boys whose rebellious mothers won't wear brassieres; not a brassiere to be found amongst her clothing — these sons suffer the most and a special shame is accorded to them. Unless, of course, they're sneaky — and most small boys are sneaky. Stealing their grandmothers' brassieres — the coveted 44 Triple Ds — and then prestige is regained, honour restored. Grandmother brassieres with cups big enough to hold two worlds. And they do, and sometimes more.

In my day it was yo-yos and marbles — the rolling and spinning of spheres. But Brassiere Season has replaced all that — an astonishing time encompassing other spring rituals as well: nine-year-old girls skipping to discover who they'll marry; twelve-year-old boys chasing everyone for kisses. And pubescent girls! They're frequently observed winking at the road crew across the street, luring them into the playground bushes. If not a workman, then an older boy passing by — and the older boys *know* to pass by. Then each girl creates a cartoon of the First Time and these pictures are displayed proudly on the outside of the school wall. A+ all around.

I'm the Playground Supervisor. Each recess and lunch I roam the fields, or stand guard at the swings and monkey bars; all the boys and girls approve of my quiet presence. I don't interfere in their spring games. "Missus, Missus," they call me. (Fondly, I like to believe.)

I'm the tallest one on the playground, the one wearing the orange reflector vest. Not an adorable body reaches above the height of my shoulders; I gaze upon a field of bobbing heads. A swaying field of rose buds bursting and bursting.

Now and again I'm honoured by a group of small boys — "Missus, Missus, this is for you!" — and shyly given a gift: a pink lace brassiere, perhaps. But never one with large cups; these they keep for themselves.

Tales from Wit's End

1. THE FIFTIES SOLUTION

They picked me up in their '56 Chevy, bringing along a thermos of martinis. A fifty-ish couple dressed and acting like this *was* the fifties. He in grey duck cut, white T-shirt, rolled jeans. His plump wife beside him on the front seat, black hair teased high, blouse collar turned up at a stiff but perky angle.

"Do you drink martinis?" she called to me gaily from the

front seat. And I had to apologize that, no, I didn't and tell my story about hating the taste of liquor because of all the lemon gin I'd consumed and then vomited as a teenager.

"When I was a teenager we ate oranges laced with Vodka and screwed in the back seats of cars," she said fondly. "Remember parking at Mt. Doug and the steamy car windows and your bum stuck to the vinyl seat? Such a lovely innocent time."

We were headed downtown to the new marriage courthouse to find their daughter a husband. And because they were required by law to have a witness, I, as their neighbour, was taken along.

"Does she know?" I asked them. "Does Tiffany know it's come to this?"

"Oh, she'll know soon enough," the girl's father smirked. He had a cigarettte stuck behind his ear. The filter had been torn off.

Their daughter was sixteen and living away from home, in another town, getting up to who knows what mischief after telling her parents: "Fuck you, I'll do what I like, smoke what I like, hang with whoever I like, most probably that crowd of losers with the purple, blue, and green hair that lives to party, smoke weed, drink rum, drop acid and do 'shrooms. My best friends in the whole world, the only ones who understand me."

Shortly after this declaration the new law had been passed

and so her parents' suffering had been shortlived. In fact, now in the car, they were downright giddy. "Imagine," Tiffany's mother said, "when Tiffany left home I thought I would die; now I'm planning family dinners, mother-daughter shopping trips, bridal showers. Oh, there's no end of possibilities. I can finally pass on my recipe book, my views about Men..."

The new law was called "The Marriage Indenture for Unruly Children Act."

Citizens groups had lobbied aged politicians, who in turn had campaigned on the platform: Marry Them Off, It Worked For Us. Once in office, the politicians soon put the program into effect. It proved highly popular with an electorate trained from birth in problem solving. "A solution at last!" they toasted one another, convinced they had successfully mined the old values; peaceful co-existence would soon be at hand.

The courtroom, when we arrived, was packed with parents and their witnesses, but not everyone was as festive as my neighbours. Many were weeping, many in obvious misery, supporting one another as they made their way to the seats. My neighbours, on the contrary, were in high spirits; already they were sharing a martini out of the plastic thermos cup and cracking remarks to those seated nearby.

"Oh, won't her little goose be cooked! Won't she be the sorry silly one!"

Before long the judge arrived and the proceedings began. A portable screen was set up beside the judge's bench and a slide projector was positioned several feet away. A government employee stood behind it. Parents or guardians were given a loose-leaf binder filled with printed information about each of the candidates — fifty young men — and a list of instructions on the bidding.

This was the girls' court; there was a similar court for unruly boys.

The courtroom lights were dimmed, the projector turned on and focussed, and the first picture flashed onto the screen: a thick-necked blond-haired boy whose name, we were told, was "Paul." The government employee read: "Paul is twenty years old, a server at his church, a help to his mother (he cuts the grass for free!) and while not what you'd call a good looker" — here the government employee aimed his pointer at Paul's Dumbo ears and acned face — "he's a good-natured, reliable boy and he's planning a career in insurance." The courtroom crowd gasped, then applauded and cheered. Many yelled out: "We want him! He's the one for us!" And so the bidding began.

When the second picture flashed on the screen — "Robert, a budding electrician" — we felt the building shake. At first we thought: *earthquake*! but the government employee reassured us on that score. It seemed a crowd of angry drug-crazed teenage girls was outside hurling their hiking boots and backpacks against the courthouse walls. We could hear them chanting: "Marriage Sucks! You Can't Make Us! We'll Wear Paper Bags to the Wedding!" Several windows had been smashed but, we were advised, the troops were in place, the threat was minimal.

"Ignore the girls," the government employee said. And everyone did. Because the courtroom crowd was more interested in discovering what Robert's sterling qualities might be. Loyalty and helpfulness, perhaps even respectfulness? But more important, maybe this inspiration who was called "Robert" had the ability to tidy a bedroom, hold a job and (dare they hope?) convince their dissenting daughters to submit, submit!

2. Battle

There's a place called "Wit's End" and I live there. It's a black place filled with guilt and accusation, practically a story book place. A place where evil queen mothers dwell, disguised as hump-backed, hand-wringing crones. Supremely ugly, eternally disgusting. Every princess knows to avoid them, has been trained from birth to revile them, these victims of makeovers in reverse, these controlling, fun-sapping mothers. Nightly we crawl into our miserable holes, lick our festering wounds and prepare for next day's battle.

The battlefield awaits. It's the breakfast table and the queen is screaming: "You've got two minutes before your ride leaves for school!!" Spit flying, eyes bulging.

The princess is serene, applying mascara before a compact mirror, her cereal uneaten. "Calm down," she growls.

Already the king is in the car honking the horn. There's a king? Yes, my god, poor thing — a hairless, skinny king, reduced to muteness, reduced to tossing his eyes at the ceiling. His eyes, these days, regularly exploding out of his head like champagne corks. The ceiling bruised, a moonscape. He's in the car now, backing it up, grimly asserting what's left of his kingness. The queen hears the threatening crunch of tire on gravel. Oh no! Her lips purse into a million wrinkles (so ugly!), her heart is racing (such uselessness), her hands are damp (wet claws). "Alright," she snaps, "miss your ride, be late for school...fail English..." *Snapping like a half-mad terrier. Snap, snap.*

The princess, still unconcerned, saunters out the door barefoot, boots in hand, stopping before the kitchen window to have a last look at her lovely self, then wanders up the drive to the retreating car. The pathetic queen on the front porch calling, "Say goodbye!" The princess deigning to speak without turning her head: "Yeah, whatever."

The face of a mother in battle is not pretty: red eyes, blotchy skin, the lines around the mouth etched in grimness. The daughter, on the other hand, is radiant — haughty, aloof, flushed with health, adept at tossing her head in pity and disdain.

Here at Wit's End, her father and I huddle, snatch anxious consultations in the bathroom, whisper over the supper table. Eye contact, imperceptible nods becoming an art form of understated communication. The battles are fast paced, the maneouvering tricky. Unpredictable mortar attacks from unpredictable demands can occur at any moment. ("Can I have that peach cooler in the fridge for breakfast?"; "I'm moving to Arizona to be a waitress so what if I'm fourteen.") Everything is liable to happen. To not happen. Morning storms are the worst, when her mood is not even civil, when demands are the strongest, responses nasty. Nasty. A word that's suddenly on our lips, hauled from the depths. A word in waiting. Amazing how it fits everything. "That was a nasty look"; "I don't like the nasty tone of your voice"; "Why must you be so *nasty*?" From the Dutch word "nestig," meaning dirty. Yes, the fighting is dirty, sly.

The queen's nose is twitching. The princess has just returned to the castle and floated through the living room where the queen is lying on the couch reading How To Deal With Your Acting Up Teenager. *There's a certain smell...*

Today the princess' hair is a shade of orange; she's wearing the king's Christmas boxer shorts — red santas on a green background — hiking boots and a yellow nylon jacket, never seen before — the kind, the queen believes, schizophrenics wear.

The queen's nose is twitching but she's about to use a new strategy, throw the princess off guard: she's going to use the word "darling." As well, following the book's advice, she's going to appear as languid and lovely as her daughter. (But there's that smell...)

"Hello darling," the queen says, her breath studied, dreamy. "Where did you get the jacket?"

"Wha?" the princess says, momentarily arrested. "Who?..."

WHAT'S TRUE, DARLING

Once upon a time, long long ago, the queen got ripped. Many many times. So many times, in fact, that this present, certain smell hovering about her daughter takes her back. But not to fourteen. At fourteen the queen remembers going to movies, having pyjama parties, curling her girlfriend's hair, giggling about boys. Her mind wasn't twisted, blown, or dulled until she was well on in age — twenty, twenty-one.

The queen is being cunning, hoping she sounds bored. "Darling," she asks, "what's that smell on you?"

A brief look of panic disturbs the princess' lovely countenance, her glassy eyes focus, stare down at the strangely relaxed queen.

The princess says, "I hate it when you're like this. You're so....so...different."

The queen smiles at her daughter's retreating back. Satisfaction. Score one for the queen. Now if only she could maintain this course...What does the book say?

The book says: "Give them responsibility for their own lives"; "Stand up for yourself"; "Assert your rights"; "Steal centre stage"; "Don't be sucked into giving them negative attention."

Alright, alright! But at times our daughter's brain power is staggering and we have to always be on the alert, scanning the skies for incoming missiles. There's the ability she has to set us up, push the right (wrong!) buttons. There's her subtle manipulations, the way she can lie so sweetly, sound so reasonable. "Ah ha! A foil!" we cry. We know that one, we've done it ourselves, we know how easy it is to lie. Heartless we were, just like she is, and conniving. Wouldn't I always try to get my way? Do anything, say anything to go to the party, date the wrong boy? And the king! The withered king who these days can't even get the dog to obey. At sixteen he had a spare set of keys made for his mother's car. The sneaky future king stealing his mother's car, roaring around town in the small hours, drunk and belligerent.

Three a.m. in the castle. Sleepless again, the queen is at her desk composing a Manifesto, thinking, "Perhaps the light approach..."

Next morning, the princess reads the Manifesto stuck to the fridge door:

1. *We are firm but reasonable parents; we don't scream (hardly ever) or hit; we simply lay down the rules. Consequences occur if rules are broken.*

2. *We are open to negotiation. We are not deaf; we are as flexible as grass in the wind.*

WHAT'S TRUE, DARLING

3. *Generally we are loving and kind. Specifically, we encounter periodic emotional disturbance with skill, patience and every street-fighting tactic we can remember.*

4. *Moment-to-moment resolutions mean nothing, although we cannot ignore the moments. Nevertheless, we will not anticipate bad moments; bad moments will not exist until they are upon us. We will live our happy fulfilled lives, thinking greater thoughts, having calm, enriching emotions, having a multitude of good moments. Breathing deeply. Counting to ten.*

5. *We will consume alcohol as required: a glass or two of sherry during skirmishes has proven helpful. A bottle of wine per weekend night is de rigeur.*

6. *Presents and money will be showered upon resident young person in adherence to Pavlovian principles: You slobber on cue, you get the treat.*

7. *Our guiding words will be: "Big Picture; Intergalactic Scheme of Things; When We're a Hundred." Hah! When you're a hundred!*

> 8. *We will make every effort to curb our pathological need to utter the words, "No, goddammit!"*

The princess tosses her shining blue hair. "Get a life," she says (would that be scorn in her voice?). "You guys are so pathetic. You think you know what's going on, but you don't."

What's going on? Booze? Drugs? Truancy? Partying at all costs? Hanging out? Scraping through school? Unprotected sex? Or none of this? Just going to movies? Having pyjama parties? Curling her girlfriend's hair? Giggling about boys?

The queen is longing for a bucket of sand in which to stick her head.

When it is said disparagingly of other queens and kings: "Oh, they don't know what's going on," the queen thinks: How wonderful! Not to know what's going on; I'd give anything for a few years of ignorance. I'd give my queendom. I'd give away my keys to the castle if only there was a suitable prince.

Would she really? Never. There's isn't a suitable prince; so far, they're all dead beat, teenage alcoholics whose descriptive vocabularies don't extend beyond the word "fuckin."

Nevertheless, the princess is howling (her hair, this time, an arresting shade of Kool Aid green), "What's the matter

WHAT'S TRUE, DARLING

with Hayden? Just because he got kicked out of school, just because he's up on drug charges."

People have stopped me on the street, pulled me aside at the grocery store, to tell me how beautiful our daughter is: "She should be a model," they say. "She's gorgeous, a knockout!" This from the ignorant mothers of sons. Or from the mothers of grown daughters. These mothers are grinning zombies now, irreversibly brain damaged; they've completely forgotten the battles, the bloodshed at the front door. Then there's the saddest group of all, the new mothers of baby girls, the ones with fear in their eyes; they look at your teenage daughter as if she were an apparition, the stuff of science fiction — a phenonemon, like leprosy, something that could never happen to them.

The queen suspects she might be having a nightmare. She's standing hands out, palms up, before a smug assembly of monarchs. These queens, she knows, consider themselves successful; their princesses do volunteer work, make the honour roll, do math without a calculator, read novels on a Friday night, iron their jeans.

The queen is trying to explain: "But my princess has an incredible mind, she's so fast and articulate. And funny! When she's in the mood she can really make us laugh; she's such a mimic. And don't forget her fashion sense; it's so...so...different. And she does love her family, I'm certain of it — the way she always comes home. Given enough time, she'll be wonderful. Right now she's wonderful-in-training..."

As the queen speaks, her words flutter to the ground like pieces of paper, like snapshots. There's that picture of the princess taken during her black period — lips, hair, nails; another of her at twelve "pretending" to smoke.

But the assembly of monarchs is angry; they're pelting the queen with family photo albums. "It won't do!" several of them are shouting.

The queen runs for cover. It's either that or being pelted to death by fond memories.

Growing up, how many times did the queen hear: "You think of no one but yourself"? She said it herself only yesterday like some condemned parrot, all teeth and spit. "You don't care if I'm injured (bruised rib from stuck door on family junker), all you want from me is to cut your hair."

Here at Wit's End the queen is holding her side in pain. *Pain!* The martyred mother howling neglect, howling the eternal subtext: "You don't love me. If you loved me, you wouldn't..." (pick anything). The princess is right, it's so pathetic, reviling, this grasping for love. A set-up for rejection.

But what the queen wants to tell her is this: "Remember

WHAT'S TRUE, DARLING

when I was the best mother in the world? And you were so direct with your love, leaving me notes on my pillow, telling me, 'I want to be just like you'? You held yourself up like a mirror, copied everything I did — the way I wore my hair, the way I walked. Oh, I was your idol! And now I've fallen. And it's me who can't abide your departure. It's me, the wicked queen, who would put you to sleep, preserve your childhood sweetness forever."

The king and queen have bought a new (1982) secondhand car. It's a sporty job with a sun roof, finely upholstered seats, doors that easily open and a tape deck that really works. It's a warm Spring evening and they're thinking about taking a spin.

The princess, late for dinner again, has just returned home. She's trudging down the driveway, shoulders bent from carrying a backpack that must weigh sixty pounds, filled as it is with every item of clothing that she owns. She's wearing a grey sweatshirt, her head covered with the hood, but it looks as if her hair sticking out the top is purple, the same colour, the queen notes, as the trailing petunias in the garden.

The king and queen are about to get into the car. Lately they've re-discovered one another, have been observed on a Friday evening dancing together in the kitchen. On several occasions now they've left notes on the dining room table that say: "Gone out for dinner. Love XO"

"Your hair — that's a pretty shade of purple," the queen says to the princess. "Where did you colour it?"

The princess glowers, "In the park." Then, narrowing her eyes: "Where are you going?"

"Out for a spin," the king says. "Want to come?"

"...No." (Was there hestiation?)

"There's leftover spaghetti in the fridge if you're hungry," the queen adds, smiling.

The king, who's looking like a UN peacekeeper in his blue beret, puts a John Lee Hooker tape in the tape deck and cranks up the volume. The queen backs up the car. In the rear-view mirror she can see the princess standing on the front porch staring. Overwhelmed with love for this rough-edged, beautiful girl, she sticks her hand out the sun roof and waves.

"Where to?" the queen hollers above "Mad Man Blues" and the king hollers back, grinning, "Anywhere. It doesn't matter. Who the hell cares?"

3. EVIL CAUCASIAN GIRL

For Anna

She calls herself "Evil Caucasian Girl." Blondisima hair in braids, multiple earrings, jeans ragged, cut at the ankle with scissors, white Doc Marten boots, striped T-shirts and men's V-neck sweaters from Value Village. She's fourteen years old and she's our daughter.

Sometimes she wears men's flannel pyjama bottoms to town with a sweatshirt and a toque. Once she wore to school a blue, short-sleeved industrial dress that came to mid-calf, buttoned down the front, and said, "Ogden Allied Services" over the breast pocket. (Add black leggings, boots, work socks and two ponytails.) She claimed that kids told her it was the most awesome thing they'd ever seen.

Her favourite accessories are little-girl plastic hair barettes in yellow and blue, a battered pink Ken & Barbie lunchkit held together with black electrical tape, and a chest full of slogan buttons found at the Sally Ann that say things like: "Us *Plus*," "We Have A Special SMILE For You," and "Bill 82." The more damaged and hokey the item, the better.

It's camp, yes, but the time it takes for something to become camp has shortened. Thus anything in neon colours, especially socks, that she loved at nine and would have died of embarassment wearing at twelve, she now covets at fourteen. She and her friends wear these socks safety-pinned above their hearts like brooches, like dangling neon flippers.

Another hot item is anything with advertising on it — but not obvious brand names like "Guess" or "Club Monaco." No, what she and her friends seek out is clothing with real advertising. Like her favourite T-shirt, found at Value Village, which has a TV scene on the front: three cats, a box of dry cat food and above this display, three large words: "Buy Meow Mix."

It's not a casual, accidental look; thought and effort go into the creation of the outfits. These girls are teenage fashion plates, adept at pulling together junk, tying it all together with binder twine and presenting themselves to the world as a kind of joyful, satiric comment.

What's wonderful about this fashion is its blithe disregard for taste and standards. I've seen girls wearing ripped satin evening gowns over grey sweat pants, or pairing dryer-shrunk Indian sweaters with taffeta skirts. A prim suit jacket in pale green linen from the sixties will have the sleeves and buttons removed and be held together with slogan buttons and safety pins. Velvet leggings are paired with ugly brown cardigans and polyester straight skirts from Goodwill. Tights have holes in them; Banlon men's socks are worn layered, mismatched and in putrid colours: mustard, bile green. Cheap black-and-white runners with crossed Velcro tops are paired with flannel boxer shorts and flared cotton print skirts. Plastic pop beads from their mother's youth find acceptance alongside homemade bead and string necklaces and strands of fake pearls — or real pearls, it wouldn't matter.

My favourite surprise was the single baby boot dangling from a backpack. This was part of an ensemble worn to an older brother's high school graduation ceremony. The rest of the outfit included blue hair, platform shoes and a shortie flannelette night gown.

What's also wonderful about this agressive, spontaneous fashion is that it would look pathetic if worn by older women. Imagine wearing the above "graduation outfit" to a board meeting or to a meeting with your daughter's teacher. Imagine wearing it grocery shopping, taking the dog for a walk, going to the dentist. You'd be reviled in seconds, phone calls would be made, you'd become the subject of serious conversations.

No, let us applaud our audacious, beautiful young women. Their fashion speaks volumes; it speaks of life, originality, novelty. It speaks of hope. Let us glory in them, in their giddy, affirming ways. Too soon, they'll be looking like the rest of us.

A Short Manual on the Care and Cultivation of Boring Relatives

For Norman Wright

1. INTRODUCTION

The cultivation of boring relatives comes from a long and noble tradition of strategies used to enhance one's self-regard in social situations. Just read your Edith Sitwell, the great English poet and essayist who documented the eighteenth-century practice of acquiring ornamental hermits. These were derelicts hired by rich people to take up residence in their gardens, on the condition that they not speak for a period of time — usually seven years. In return for food and rough shelter, the derelicts would be there in the garden, ornamentally, when the house guests were brought by for a stroll before dinner.

Today, of course, things are different. How to carry on in the face of the world's disapproval has become the pressing question. Certainly, at this stage of the century we have to be more subtle, more devious in our bids for self-glorification than our predecessors — there are now fewer and fewer ways in which we can achieve personal "wonderfulness" without being exposed as exploiters. So it is with great relief that we have discovered the importance of the Boring Relative, whose cultivation is such a harmless pursuit and, truly, one of the few areas of exclusivity left to us. It's so easy to own things — objects, gadgetry — but an authentic Boring Relative is hard to come by. You must be born into it or marry into it. There is no other way.

WHAT'S TRUE, DARLING

2. THE MANY VARIETIES OF BORING RELATIVE

There are many varieties of the Boring Relative in existence and new varieties are being discovered every day, perhaps even as you read this. It is an exciting field of study. As a beginning student, though, you may wish to limit yourself to cultivation of one or two of the more common sub-species.

What follows, therefore, is a partial list. It is partial because thorough lists are depressing — including *everything* in a list is a stifling thing to do and, well, it's something a Boring Relative would do. It's rigid, there's nothing creative or dangerous about it, nothing is left to chance. Keep this in mind the next time you make a list. Be sure to leave things out. Do this on purpose. It is charming to dabble in chaos. It means you have more important things to do than fret endlessly over trivial decisions — what you're going to eat next Tuesday, for example.

A. *One-Dimensionals*

One-Dimensionals have got one story to tell and they'll tell it to anyone who even gives an appearance of listening. And they'll tell it endlessly, year in, year out, and as many times in the course of a gathering as they're able, often several times to the same person. The more menacing of this species spend their lives searching for a single viewpoint to live by and then years laying on the mud and concrete of rigid thinking to keep their viewpoint unshakeable. Diversionary fun can be had by pairing One Dimensionals of opposing views. The resulting fireworks display can add interest to some settings — for example, when your own dinner-party brawling no longer carries the same, exciting punch.

B. The Eternal Mommy

The Eternal Mommy is your relative, male or female, who is burdened with advice and the need to impart it to all and sundry, whether it is asked for or not; they always have at their fingertips the right course of action for any situation. Whether or not there is a problem doesn't seem to matter; they have solutions for everything, if only you'd listen.

This special breed of Boring Relative is expert at diagnosing your vague medical complaints and it's clear they've read their *Merck's Manual of Diseases* from cover to cover because the "C" word is never far from their lips. Frequently used phrases in this regard are: "all over in a matter of weeks," "lightning speed," "spread like wildfire," "the size of a baseball" and "showed up on the X-ray."

C. Boring Pets

The attendance of a Boring Pet can add miles of texture to any function and you will be praised highly for including them — their presence borders on the bizarre. Boring Pets are always, for some reason, dogs, and the smaller the animal the more boring its status. Large athletic dogs do not make good Boring Pets and neither do cats, who are simply too indifferent. Sometimes budgies will qualify but only indirectly, as the subject, say, of a One-Dimensional's story. A miniature-breed lap dog makes the best Boring Pet (a beribboned Poodle named "Lovey" comes to mind). To qualify as boring, the animal should be spoilt, fat and nasty, able to perform at least one trick — beg, kiss Mommy — but nothing too intelligent. If it gets loose, it should never come when called.

D. *Child Bores*

Child Bores are the dread of all social gatherings but sometimes their attendance is unavoidable, such as when their mother marries "Uncle John." Child Bores are virulent weeds and their toxicity seems to be at its worst when there is only one of them in attendance. Two Child Bores can often be bribed to "go outside and play," although a pack of Child Bores rampaging through your garden is a frightening thing. In general, Child Bores do not understand the word "no." Nor do they understand disapproving gestures from strangers. The only thing they seem to understand comes from their hapless parents: "Have another cookie, Sweetie," and "I'll buy you one later but only if you're good." "One," of course, can be anything from a Nintendo machine to a dude ranch but "later" is always within the hour, which means relief is in sight — they will soon be leaving. The usual age of a Child Bore is between two and twelve. Before age two, they are excused as babies. After thirteen, you needn't worry, as these sullen critics will rarely make an appearance, indeed they would rather die first. The only time a teenager will attend an adult function is if they're being punished.

E. Heaps

A venomous derivative of the genus Uriah. Can be found clustered weed-like with other Heaps at any gathering. Extremely poor mixers. Heaps, if catered to, will monopolise any function and, if they are allowed to dominate, your party will soon become as dull and as plodding as they are. There is an overpowering quality of lethargy which attends their presence and seems to radiate outwards. Sometimes it can overtake a whole group of hitherto unknown sympathisers, and before you know it, everyone is glassy-eyed and yawning — a rapid and dismal end to the festivities is about to occur.

F. Family Feebes

Family Feebes are hopeless, feeble individuals who can't seem to get on in life. They deserve our support and understanding because they were born under the great "Un" star — unsuccessful, unlucky, unhappy, uninspired, unfortunate. A kind of low-grade tragedy cloud seems to hover outside their doors: their dogs get cruel diseases, and their trucks, houses and love lives are perpetually breaking down. They spend any money they get hold of on sad stupid things, like one-hundred-dollar garden gnomes when they're on welfare and the rent's due. But we can't be too hard on them because they're our brother, father, sister and they're bringing the kids for supper on Sunday, having just left Joe or Shelley for the fifth time in two years.

G. Dead Boring Relatives

There are two kinds of Dead Boring Relatives: those who are "dead" from the neck up but still able to walk through your kitchen door, block your driveway with their cars and arrive two hours late for the turkey dinner; and those who are dead and buried but in body only, as in: just when you'd thought you'd heard the last of old Uncle Raymond's endless stories (forty-five years battling eczema) there's his wife retelling all the flaky details.

3. GENERAL ENVIRONMENTAL CONDITIONS

Establishing the "right" environmental conditions for the cultivation of Boring Relatives means hosting the right kind of gathering; there are a number of inflexible rules which must be adhered to.

Rule #1 : Formal Invitations

Send them. Everyone, including the least boring amongst us, is susceptible to the thrill of finding a personally addressed envelope tucked between the Sears flyers and the Visa bill. Remember: time, date, place — a lifeline, an anchor, a rope to the future.

Rule #2: Clearly Defined Events

Boring Relatives do not understand theme parties, stomach clubs or taking-down-the-Christmas-tree-in-June parties. The event must be traditional and conservative with a long and proven history of dullness — for example, Spring Teas, Christmas Cheer and Open House.

Rule #3: Large Events

Specialize in them. Until you are skilled at combining boring and non-boring guests, never, never have less than twenty people in attendance. It's just too dangerous: There you'll be, fifteen of you, sitting on kitchen chairs in a kind of desolate wagon-train circle around the living room, and no one will be saying much of anything except, "Congratulations, you've just managed to host the most boring evening in existence!"

Rule #4: Bland Food

Field studies have shown that Boring Relative attendance is directly correlated to the consumption of white cake, asparagus rolls made of soft, white bread, and jellied salads in alarming shades of pink and green.

4. FOUNDATION PLANTING

Since one of the primary purposes of Boring Relative cultivation is to enhance the individual practitioner and to tone down his or her more unattractive traits — an unsightly barrenness of spirit, for example — it is generally agreed that foundation planting is in order. This can be accomplished with the acquisition of five good One-Dimensionals arranged carefully around the cultivator like foliage around a rose. You cannot hope to proceed to the exotic blends until you have mastered foundation planting. For the beginner, start with One-Dimensionals, add an Eternal Mommy and perhaps a Boring Pet for a creditable first effort. Become comfortable with this arrangement before you move on to more exotic blends.

5. BORING RELATIVE SURVIVAL SKILLS: HOW TO AVOID BECOMING A BORING RELATIVE BEFORE YOUR TIME

1. Always reinforce the attitudes and opinions of anyone in your extended family regardless of their logic, at least within earshot.

2. Keep the above relatives in psychic paralysis with frequent doses of unvarnished truth, untruth and emotional blackmail.

3. Practise the ancient art of emotional distancing: *I don't care. I don't care. I don't care.*

4. Read. Cultivate a secret, imaginative life. Stretch your mind beyond the mundane. Dabble in Dada.

5. Never attend family functions if you believe that they are either (a) too filled with emotions and meaning, or (b) absolutely boring.

6. AFTERWORD

A time may come when you seek out the state of Relative Boredom for yourself, like a Buddhist monk, and so the categories just listed may be of some help. Perhaps you're sick of hosting dinners or you're down on your luck, and a good meal — one that is free of organizational responsibility — would be nice. Maybe you're world weary, filled with ennui, more bored with yourself than boring to others. Maybe you feel physically sick when someone sprints by you shouting, "Okay! Who's ready for another fun-fix?" Whatever the reason, becoming a Boring Relative can, for some, be an extremely esoteric exercise. As a result, your life will suddenly become ponderous with meaning. This is a state *achieved*, like grace, and vastly different from life as experienced by the "found," or naturally occurring, Boring Relative. Unfortunately, it's difficult to distinguish the garden variety from the philosophical, except for something about the eyes of the latter — and a certain bemused and ever-present grin.

Little Zerotta

IF DOGS WERE MEN, WE'D HAVE IT IN SPADES for our Zero. We've got heaps of dogs hanging about the place but marrying men are a scarce commodity. It used to be so easy, with her having the use of puny Billy Street, but suddenly this arrangement isn't good enough. Ever since she discovered *Bride Magazine* amongst the stack of papers in that hovel Billy Street calls home, there's been no living with her.

"I'm going to have a wedding in white," Zero's now telling everyone, all sharp-faced and eager-eyed. "I want someone

I can dress up and put in my very own living room; someone I can vacuum around and dust while he's watching TV then carry off to bed come midnight. I want Alfred Angelo Dream Maker."

She thinks Alfred Angelo's the name of the man on page twenty-three of *Bride Magazine*, a dandy looking man with slicked-back hair wearing a black tuxedo. Be about nineteen or twenty, not a whisper more. "Honey," we keep telling her, "Alfred Angelo's the name of the company that makes wedding dresses and that magazine man is just a model."

But love's stunted Zero's mind; every puff of intelligence she ever had has caught the last bus out of town. Zero won't see reason. When we tell her the truth about the picture she covers her ears and screams: "Not true, not true." She's thrown chairs and dishes at us, upturned the supper table calling the lot of us dream wreckers, malignant dashers of hope and better days.

One time Grandma caught her practising the writing of her new name and this was alarming, as if Little Zerotta was no longer good enough for her, now it had to be Zero Dream Maker, Mrs. Dream Maker, Mrs. Alfred A. Dream Maker. She was writing these names over and over and smiling like she was in a trance. Zero with her emotions all over the map, running wild and mean because of love.

Pops says, "We went through this once already, when she was fifteen, and now she's twenty-nine; I don't know if I can live through another round."

"Well, it's definitely love," Grandma announced at supper. "No doubt about it, we'll have to find her a man." And we put down our knives and forks and stared sadly at our Zero.

Talk about catastrophe! We can't figure out who besides Billy Street would marry Zero. Beautiful to us, she is, but truly, not much of a tender morsel. Mean and wiry, actually. And yes, yes, we'd be the first to agree that nobody's-at-home Billy Street isn't the kind of man you'd find in the pages of *Bride Magazine*, living dirty and disgusting the way he does in his hovel. Not to be unkind, but when a fact's shoving itself in your face it's hard to wax conceptual. Billy Street doesn't look the least like the man on page twenty-three of February's *Bride Magazine* and that's who Zero's wanting. Someone who looks like that. But everytime we try to picture Billy Street inside a black wedding suit, his long hair all washed and puffy and him wearing shoes, we can't stand up for laughing. Billy Street's been wearing them red thongs for so long they're about moulded to his feet. And that red-and-black flannel shirt got put on his back out of a dumpster in 1977 and hasn't been off his skinny body since.

So Billy Street can take a hike as far as Zero's concerned. And it's pitiful to see. Damn heartbreaking, the way he's been hanging around our mobile home with all the dogs out front, that Safeway cart of his parked across the patch of grass like he's conducting a roadblock.

"I ain't moving till Zero comes back to my shed," he's been shouting to Grandma.

And Grandma's been shouting back: "Get lost Billy Street. Face the music. Zero's fallen in love with a magazine picture and there's no way on earth you'll ever look like Alfred Angelo in *Bride Magazine*. You had your chance, she's moving on to greater things."

Greater things? We've had to sit Grandma down and ask her this: "Where are we going to find a man who looks like Alfred Angelo?"

"Put an ad in the paper?"

"We tried that, no one replied."

"Make one out of cardboard?" Grandma offers.

"What I'd be more worried about is The Business," Pops says, thundering into the scene the way he always does, putting the exact right spin on the situation. Of course, The Business! Little Zerotta, Champion Fire-Eater! Ever since Zero fell in love with a magazine picture, The Business has gone to hell.

We're constantly in a sweat now trying to get her into costume and up on stage, and all because she won't stop looking at page twenty-three of February's *Bride Magazine* and moaning about wanting a normal life — a husband and a set of dishes in the suburbs.

"Honey," we plead, "put aside your magazine for a while, just long enough to do the show; there's an audience waiting, people have paid money to see you. Pops has even sewn some new red and silver sequins onto your costume and Grandma's washed and fluffed your feather plume. Everyone's in place. Your brother Gerald the Giant is manning the spot light. Do the show for Gerald. You know how agitated he gets when he can't play his part."

Sometimes Zero does the show, sometimes she doesn't. And when she doesn't — it's Grandma into the costume and up on stage, which is game of her. She hasn't performed the fire-eating act for over twenty years, but never mind. She says, "You've got to do what you've got to do. And if it's for The Family Business…"

The rest of us hoping the audience won't hear the awful belching coming out of Grandma's mouth. And then it's dimming the lights to fool the audience about Zero's replacement. Or rather trying to convince Gerald to dim the lights, because Gerald hates change, he's as stubborn as a mountain. "*Why? Why?*" he screams, and even when we patiently explain, still he bawls, "*No way, I've always used the bright yellow spotlight for the first trick and then the orange and then the pink and I'm not changing things now, not for anyone.*"

The audience by now shuffling in their seats, made nervous by the shouting. And then seriously alarmed when Billy Street appears at the back of the tent wearing a creased black suit, his hair slicked back like Alfred Angelo. And he's walking on his hands towards the stage, hollering, "Look Zero, I'm Billy Street the Upside Down Dancer. Now we can get married and be a team." And Zero peeking out from behind the curtain and getting a smirk on her face, falling down laughing.

And then it's Pops flinging up his arms in disgust and telling the rest of us backstage, "That's it, I've had it, I'm divorcing the lot of you. I'm moving to a cabin in the woods and I'm never coming out." Tearing off his baby blue jockstrap and angrily shoving his silver lamé cape into the garbage. "The Family Business can go to hell!"

The last time The Family Business went to hell was when we ended Grandma's career as Little Zerotta. Oldpops was alive then; he was Cinatus the Fire Eating Contortionist, whose specialty was eating fire while dragging his body along the stage like a snake. Grandma and Oldpops were a team, but they were getting on and their timing had gone, accidents were occuring. They dropped the torches; several times they set the curtains on fire. And they insisted on practising their tricks inside the mobile home; there were burn marks everywhere — on the carpet, the sofa, their costumes. After they burned down the tent, we convinced them to retire and let Zero, who was only nine at the time, take over. She was a huge success. Audiences loved her pale hair and spindly legs and the way the torch was bigger than she was. As she grew taller we had to make the torch larger to keep up the little girl illusion.

Pops was delighted with the way things had turned out. Now he didn't have to take over centre stage and resurrect himself as the Human Claw-Hammer (using his teeth to pull spikes from a two-inch plank); he could act as Zero's assistant. And I was delighted because I could hang up my outfit for Madame Rice the Weeping Wonder (exhibitions of tearful sobbing) and concentrate on running the business. And Gerald the Giant didn't care who was out front as long as he could man the lights.

But that was then. Now we had a new catastrophe.

I found Pops behind the mobile home sitting on the old couch having a smoke. He still had his make-up on — red lips, blue-and-silver eye shadow. There must have been ten dogs, all sizes, crowded around him, wagging their tails, nudging his arms and legs with their noses. Poor Pops! He looked so sad and dejected.

"What are we going to do without Little Zerotta?" he said when he saw me. It was plain he'd been crying. "She's impossible and I'm sick of this Alfred Angelo business; she doesn't care two hoots about fire-eating; it's clear to me she's about to hang up her torch for good. And I can't go on stage. I'm nearly sixty, Mona. I can't pull nails with my teeth anymore — hell, I don't have any teeth. And what about you? No one's going to pay to see a fat, middle-aged woman get up on a stage and bawl her eyes out when they can see it for free on Oprah. And then there's Gerald and he's useless. We only gave him that Giant name so's he'd feel a part of things. What's going to happen when he doesn't have a show to light? He'll get seriously mad, Mona, that's what will happen; he'll start breaking things and roughing up the audience."

I didn't know what to say to Pops; the show has been our life.

One of the dogs, a small retreiver, gave Pop's leg a nudge with her paw. We looked at her. The dog started making noises. "Huh row," she said.

Pops stopped sniffling. "That sounded like 'Hello,'" he said, suddenly interested. "Hello," he said to the dog. "Say it again, little girl. Hello."

The dog said, "Huh row row row," and Pops laughed.

I took out my notebook and started writing: Little Angelo the Amazing Talking Dog.

I liked the look of it and was writing it again when Zero and Billy Street came running towards us holding hands. "Guess what?" Zero shrieked. "Billy and me made up. He's gonna buy me a subscription to *Homes & Gardens* if I keep fire-eating long enough for him to get his chiropractor ticket. And then we'll get married and buy a condo and a Land Rover and a Dirt Devil and just everything."

Billy Street stood beside her grinning like the moron he is. "That's right," he said, pulling at his filthy plaid shirt.

"This here dirt and grime's a thing of the past."

Pops looked wearily from the talking dog to Zero and Billy Street. "That's it," he said, "I give up, I'm throwing in the towel."

And then everyone laughed. Because that's what Pops always says during a catastrophe and it means nothing, nothing at all.

Tic-Tac-Doe

BECAUSE WE COULDN'T SELL OUR 1980 PEUGEOT — it had a blown head gasket — I phoned a number advertised in the community paper: "Tic-Tac-Doe Cabinets. Will trade kitchen cabinets for something of value." I told the man on the line that we wanted bathroom cabinets and tiling in the area around the tub. If he could do this we would give him the car.

"All it needs is a head gasket," I said. "And it's in beautiful shape. The body's great, a dark wine colour. It's got a plush interior and a sun roof. It looks like a Mercedes."

He said he was interested and we arranged a time for him to come and look at the job.

"What's your name?" I asked.

"Tickner. Daryl Tickner."

Two nights later, Daryl Tickner drove up in a 1972 Plymouth, beige, with large patches of rust around the rear wheels. Daryl was in his late thirties, tall but solidly built, wearing black cowboy boots. He had a long thin pony tail which hung over his plaid jacket. The jacket was dirty, with smears of oil on the sleeves and chest. He wore a diamond stud in his left ear.

He took off his boots when he came in the house, then looked at the bathroom. The sink area consisted of a platform of white melamine board, a curtain (green and yellow flowers) hung in place of cabinet drawers, and the floor was covered in lime green tiles, a colour that for some reason I had loved deeply in 1984. To complete the sordid effect, the sheeting around the bathtub was cracked and warped; black mould was growing around the edges.

Of this Daryl said, "It'll have to be replaced before we can put on tile. I'll have to rip it out and put up half-inch plywood first." He sounded disgusted.

He put his boots back on and went outside with my husband to look at the car. It had been sitting in the driveway for a year and a half and one of the rear tires was flat. Daryl opened a front door and peered inside the car. Then he looked under the hood. It was impossible to guess what he was thinking.

I watched the men from the vestibule window. They walked solemnly around the car several times then leaned against the hood and had a smoke.

Then they came inside. This time Daryl left his boots on.

"Nothing else wrong with the car besides the head gasket?" he asked.

"No."

"All right," he said, "I'll do it but I'll need three hundred dollars for materials. I've got to get the cabinet top and the wood to build the cabinets. I'll trade my labour for the car. You pick up the tile you want for the tub. Soon as we get that, I'll have my partner out here laying her up."

He wanted the three hundred dollars up front. We balked.

"I can't be putting out money like that," he said, "what with a family to feed."

"A family to feed, yes, of course," we said anxiously. And agreed to his terms. How much longer would the car sit in the driveway unless we did? How much longer would the rot and mould around the bathtub continue to disgrace us?

Before we gave him the money, though, we wanted a reference.

"No problem," Daryl said. And gave us the name and phone number of a Dr. Donnelly. "I put in his kitchen. Call him tonight if you want."

It was a Monday night.

"You get the tile by the weekend and the cash to me tomorrow morning and we can sign the contract. The bathroom will be finished this time next week. But I don't work Sunday," he added. "I never work on the Lord's day."

After Daryl left, I found the number of Dr. Donnelly in the phone book. He was listed at a clinic on the other side of town. His phone number was different from the one Daryl gave us — probably his home phone, I reasoned. My husband did the phoning. He was grinning when he finished the call. "Dr. Donnelly says Daryl doesn't have hemorrhoids. And he said he did the work okay, there weren't any problems."

"So there really is a Dr. Donnelly?"

"Must be. He's in the book."

"Good," I said. "I'm sure Daryl needs the work. And if he's hooked into a church..."

"That's the oldest con in the book," my husband said, "Guys talking about the Lord. That's what sucks people in. Especially old people. They think it means reliable, honest, trustworthy. Pretty soon they're having their roofs redone or their houses painted when they don't need it. And then it's thousands of dollars later. All because of a line about the

WHAT'S TRUE, DARLING

Lord. I knew a guy called Ray who did this all the time. With him it was septic tanks. Digging them up for nothing."

But we went ahead with the deal.

The next morning I drove the forty miles to Daryl's house. It was ten-thirty when I got there. A shabby house, white with light blue trim, at the end of a cul de sac. Two rusted cars in the driveway. An old blue pickup truck parked outside on the road.

After several minutes, a man answered the door. Late forties, skinny, in his undershirt, unshaven.

"Sorry, I was asleep. Didn't hear the bell."

He asked me in.

"Daryl's out back. I'll get him."

"This is my partner Ray," Daryl said, introducing me to the man when he came in. "Ray Tacowski — the 'Tac' of Tic-Tac-Doe." There were tattoos of snakes on both of Ray's forearms. I noticed most of Daryl's bottom teeth were missing.

We sat at the kitchen table. Ray had disappeared. There were children's drawings tacked on the wall and more drawings and notices on the fridge door. On the kitchen counter were several boxes of breakfast cereal lined up neatly, a jar of instant coffee, a jar of Coffee Mate. Looking into the dining room I could see a china cabinet filled with crystal wine glasses, china plates, cups and saucers. The place looked reassuring, like an established household.

Everything was business like. Daryl had a contract ready for me to sign. With a clause that said the contract was void if the work wasn't completed within thirty days.

He showed me plans for someone else's kitchen. "Doing cabinets in exchange for a motor home," he said, "but I'll do your bathroom first."

I gave him six fifty-dollar bills. He gave me a receipt.

"I'll be out tomorrow to take measurements," he said.

"What time?"

"After supper."

Later I told my husband: "I met the 'Tac' of Tic-Tac-Doe Cabinets. Ray Tacowski. Wonder if it's the same Ray you knew?"

"Fat guy? Bald?"

"No. He's skinny, got hair. Brown and greasy."

"Doesn't sound like the same Ray."

"Looks like an alcoholic. Shakes when he walks."

"Figures. They're both probably on step one of a nineteen-step recovery program."

"Could be," I said. "Which is why we've got to hang in there. People on recovery programs need our support."

"Mmmm."

"Anyway, they've got the money now."

"You didn't give them cash did you?"

WHAT'S TRUE, DARLING

"That's what he wanted."

"Jesus."

"What difference would a cheque make now? We're already committed. It'll be all right, you'll see. His house didn't look fly-by-night. It looked like a place where people lived."

"So what? You think crooks don't live in houses?"

"If you're so worried why'd you agree to the deal?"

"Because it's the only way we'll get rid of the car," my husband said.

That night we drove into town. We spent two hundred dollars on five boxes of white tile, a fifty pound sack of mortar, a tub of grout and a new toilet seat.

My husband stacked the materials on the front porch.

We saw Daryl three days later, Friday night.

"Jeez, sorry about the last few days," he said. "My son's been sick. I couldn't go anywhere."

We said we understood.

He took the bathroom measurements. "What colour countertop?" he asked.

"White."

"I'll have to order it. You wouldn't want pink, would you? I've got some real nice pink."

"No," we said, "we want white."

A week later I phoned Daryl.

"Where have you been?"

"Jeez, I should have phoned. I got the flu. I been so sick I couldn't get out of bed. It's really put me behind. Remember I told you about my son being sick? I got it from him. Last night I had a temperature of a hundred and three."

I said I understood. And hoped he'd get well.

Another week went by.

"I keep trying to go to work," Daryl said when I phoned again, "but this bug's really laid me out. I've had to cancel the motor home deal. All I do is sleep. But I've ordered the counter top. Should be here next week."

When I told my husband he said, "Flu, my ass. He's stalling till the thirty days are up on the contract. Then the deal will fall through. He'll have the three hundred bucks and we'll have dick. And just try to get the money back from him then. I know these guys. This is the way they operate."

"I wonder if Dr. Donnelly is the 'Doe' of Tic-Tac-Doe Cabinets?" I said. Picturing another guy like Daryl and Ray — maybe the janitor at Dr. Donnelly's office. With the name of Don. Hanging around waiting for the call from pigeons like us. Picturing the Three Stooges with a sinister twist.

I called Daryl twice the following week. The first time he told me the countertop had come in and that he'd been working on the cabinets. "But the damnedest thing happened today," he said, "a bearing on my saw broke. If I can't fix it I'll have to get a new saw."

The other call was 10 a.m. on a Saturday morning. A woman answered the phone. When I asked for Daryl she said, "He's in bed."

I started to tell her why I was calling: "It's about the cabinets...I was wondering if he's bringing them out today."

"Just a minute," she said, sounding annoyed, and went and got him.

"Yeah, they're just about finished," Daryl said when he finally got on the line. "I'll bring them out on Monday and we can wrap the whole job up in two days."

It was eight days later, on a Sunday, that we saw Daryl. After several more calls from me, he said he could see I was getting antsy. "I don't usually work on the Lord's day," he said, "but for you I'll make an exception; I'll come out after church and we'll get started."

"What time will that be?"

"After lunch. But I don't have the cabinets together," he said.

"Bring the countertop anyway," I said, thinking at least we'd have something to show for our money.

At three he drove up.

"Sorry I'm late," he said. "But the damnedest thing happened. I was getting gas beside the Waddling Dog Inn and who should I bump into but my lawyer. So we went and had a beer. Haven't seen him in a coon's age."

The countertop was in the back seat of his car. White. It looked okay. He stopped when he was carrying it into the house to have a look at the tile on the front porch. "That's the tile, eh?" he said. And sighed.

Then he got to work tearing the bathroom apart. He pulled the sheeting away from the tub. "Look at that," he said, almost delighted. "You've got an ant's nest in there."

We put on the bathroom fan because the mildew smell was so bad. Moments later he asked me for a cold drink. Not long after this, my husband asked me for a bandaid. He said Daryl had a rash on his hand that he wanted to cover.

The tearing apart, the sawing, the hauling drywall outside continued for an hour. I was making supper. My husband was helping Daryl. Before long he came into the kitchen and said Daryl was sitting on the edge of the bathtub holding his jaw. "He's got a toothache."

Minutes later, I met Daryl in the hallway. He looked miserable. His hand was still holding his jaw. "It's killing me," he said. "I've got to go."

I said I understood.

After he'd gone, my husband said, "At least he's left his tools. He'll have to come back and finish the job now."

We looked at the tools: a wooden tool box, a battery driven drill, a hand saw, tape measures, a level and three new hammers with the price tags still on — all $49.95.

"He probably bought those with our three hundred dollars," my husband said.

He'd left his jacket, too, thrown on the bathroom floor.

The only problem was that now the bathroom was completely useless. Daryl had disconnected the bolts to the toilet and the bathtub was filled with mouldy debris from the walls. The pink insulation on the walls was exposed and the bathroom floor was splattered with used drywall mud. This meant we had to use the toilet in the basement. "We paid three hundred dollars for some guy to come and trash our bathroom," my husband said.

I left the sheets on the floor covering the route from the front door to the bathroom. Because I was certain we'd see Daryl tomorrow.

I should have known better: the toothache. He'd seen his dentist, he was on antibiotics, he'd had to stop four times on the drive home from our place because of the pain, the pain was so bad he could hardly see, he'd had a temperature of a hundred and three.

"What? A hundred and three again?" my husband said.

"So maybe he's sickly," I said. "But he's trying. You can tell he's trying. He says he'll be out tomorrow for sure."

At 8:15 the next morning, Daryl phoned: "I'll be out later this morning. I'm just finishing up the cabinets."

When my husband phoned from work to see if Daryl had

shown up I told him about the early call. "8:15 in the morning," I said, impressed.

"Up at 8:15?" my husband said. "He must have shit the bed."

At three-thirty, I phoned Daryl.

"What happened?"

"You won't believe my day," he said. "But I won't bore you with the details. We'll get it done tomorrow. That's a promise."

That night my husband said: "I'm going to phone him up, tell him to keep the three hundred dollars and I'll keep his tools. And I'll finish the goddamned bathroom myself."

I managed to calm him down. "Confrontation won't get us anywhere," I said. "And who's going to buy a bunch of tools, most of which are used? The only way we're going to get those cabinets is by playing along with him, waiting it out. We already have the countertop and we haven't signed over the car yet. If we just hang in there a little longer, I'm sure it will work out. He's obviously learning how to be reliable."

"This is just like social work," said my husband who works with the behaviour problems at the local middle school.

Meanwhile there was the mildew smell coming from the bathroom. And the three a.m. treks downstairs in the dark to pee.

WHAT'S TRUE, DARLING

Two days later, Daryl and Ray showed up with the cabinets. It was the first time Ray had been to the house. The delay in their arrival was because they'd had to borrow a truck. ("My brother's got my Aerostar.") It was six-thirty. I'd phoned their place at five. A kid had answered the phone: "No he's not here, he'll be back in an hour."

"Is he delivering cabinets?" I had asked, hoping I didn't sound too desperate.

"Just a minute," the kid had said. I heard a woman's voice in the background, then the kid told me uncertainly, "Yeah, he's delivering cabinets." I pictured Daryl sitting at his kitchen table and mouthing to the kid: *Tell her I'm not home.* And eating his supper of canned spaghetti and beer and laughing.

So I was happy and relieved when they actually showed up. They carried the cabinet frames into the house, puffing and laughing. Ray was wearing a T-shirt that said "Crazy Gringo."

"No doors or drawers yet," Daryl said happily, "but they're just about finished." They'd brought two sheets of plywood as well, for nailing up around the tub, and left them propped against the house. They were in a good mood, pleasant, talkative. Proud of themselves, it seemed, for actually delivering the goods.

They stayed long enough to bring the cabinets into the hallway and tell us they'd be back tomorrow. Which, miraculously, they were, managing to work three straight hours and arriving only four hours later than they had said. This day was their most productive; they nailed up the plywood and got the cabinets in place. I made them coffee, telling them I'd be back in fifteen minutes, I had to pick up my son from school. When we returned they were sitting inside the Peugeot. Daryl was in the driver's seat, his hands on the steering wheel. It looked like they were pretending they were driving somewhere.

After that, the pace picked up. Slightly. We got two more two-hour workdays out of them. When Daryl said they'd be out midmorning, I blithely told my husband that it would be mid-afternoon. And it was. Unloading the cabinet doors from his car trunk, Daryl said, "I've nearly had a nervous breakdown doing this job." And I said, "So have we!"

During these days Daryl and Ray laughed together while they worked. And they had long conversations about the right way to hammer in the cabinets and even one about a woman who wore coke bottle glasses: "You could dump a pot of potatoes over her head and she wouldn't know," Ray said. "Jeez, it'd blow my mind if I couldn't see." Daryl sang hymns while he worked: "Rock of Ages" and "Onward Christian Soldiers."

The toilet had been removed by now and sat on blocks

on the front porch, like an old car that would one day be worked on — our toilet rudely exposed for the neighbours to see: its shocking white body, its sad, empty bowl. I recited to my husband the first lines of a poem by Russell Edson: "The toilet slides into the living room on it's track of slime demanding to be loved…"

I found myself happy to see Daryl and Ray when they'd finally arrive for their daily two hours. The bathroom was being worked on, something was happening. Ray turned out to be a talker; he told me to get rid of the English ivy in our yard because it was killing the pear tree. He said he'd been in the tree business for fifteen years (removing trees that didn't need removing?) and said he knew what he was talking about. When Ray wasn't telling me about his past businesses (trees, roofs, windows), sawing bits of plywood, or cutting tiles, he was rolling cigarettes, playing tag with the dog or using the bathroom downstairs. He was polite but very nervous. I noticed that when he sat on the front porch smoking he couldn't keep his legs still, they shook of their own accord. But the work progressed. Daryl seemed quite moved and said thank you when I told him that the job was looking good.

But this pair of two-hour workdays turned out to be our Golden Age with Tic-Tac-Doe Cabinets. It's true Daryl and Ray finally got the tile on the walls, but it was clear they didn't know what they were doing. The tiles were placed crookedly, mortar was splattered on the ceiling, the bathtub, the floor. And many of the tiles were chipped. When my husband pointed this out, neither of them knew about tile cutters; they'd broken over two dozen tiles trying to fit them around the faucets. And then they started grumbling loudly to each other about all the time the job was taking. "We're almost doing this for free," Daryl said, and Ray said, "Yeah, it's like doing a welfare job."

They never did grout the tile like they said they would; they simply didn't show up. My husband finished the job. Grouting, hanging cupboard doors, replacing cracked tiles, replacing the toilet (it finally being hugged by him on the return trip to the bathroom — oh happy toilet!), and cleaning up the appalling mess they'd left. My husband figured he spent about nineteen hours all told. But the thing was, we still had their tools. Added to Daryl's collection was Ray's: another electric hand saw, three more hand drills, hammers, screwdrivers and an impressive assortment of nails. We also found Daryl's copy of our signed contract with him and his rough sketch of our bathroom. We put everything in the trunk of the Peugeot, which, of course, remained ours. While they were here, they'd never once asked to start it up.

To finish the bathroom we bought some stick-on tiles for

the floor, black and white, and two new black towels. The new toilet seat was installed and a new white shower curtain hung from a new chrome curtain rod. A coat of white semi-gloss paint was applied. The bathroom looked dazzling, even with the crooked tiles. We kept going in there just to marvel at the transformation, to gape and gasp; at last we had a bathroom where our guests would be proud to pee. The only thing missing was one of the doors beneath the sink; Daryl hadn't brought it with him on his last visit.

The final call to Daryl occurred over this issue. It was a Tuesday morning, two weeks after their botched tile job and a full three months after we'd signed the thirty-day contract.

My husband told him we wanted the cabinet door and asked Daryl when he planned to deliver it. But Daryl started complaining. He said he'd been misled (his word) about the job, and my husband said that, as a contractor, Daryl should have known what he was getting into. Then my husband mentioned the five hours it had taken him to do the grouting and Daryl said, "Bullshit, ask anybody in the trade, it's only a half-hour job." After this exchange, "screw you" and "goddamn" started flying. Also: "you're full of shit," "blow it out your ass" and "who the hell do you think you're talking to?" And then an angry Daryl said he'd be right out with the door and my husband shouted, "The sooner the fucking better!"

That was six months ago. We haven't heard from Daryl or Ray since. And we still have their tools. And the car. Everyone who visits us hears this story and then has a look at the tools in the back of the Peugeot. Estimates of their worth run anywhere from five hundred to two thousand dollars, well in excess of the value of the car. Someone suggested that maybe they were stolen. And everyone gives us advice as to what we should do next: sell the tools at a garage sale; send Daryl and Ray a registered letter telling them that we're storing their tools at $2.50 a day; phone up Dr. Donnelly and tell him to never again recommend Tic-Tac-Doe Cabinets; consult a lawyer. It's not unlikely that we'll have the tools with us for the next several years.

But it's the car that's really the problem: we can't seem to get rid of it. It clings to us like our forlorn toilet demanding to be loved. It costs too much to fix, which is why we've been driving a 1979 Ford Fairmont for the last two years, ever since the Peugeot's head gasket blew on the Pat Bay Highway two days before Christmas. We don't think Daryl and Ray still have a claim on the car because they didn't fulfil the terms of the contract.

So really this story is one long classified ad: "Peugeot for sale, beautiful body, needs head gasket." If anyone reading this is interested in owning the car, we'll let it go for two hundred dollars. Failing that, we have an idea for another ad: "Wanted: door-to-door vacuum salesmen. Will trade valuable luxury car for state of the art vacuum cleaner. Only the desperate need apply."

Weird Pets

For Sara

THERE'S THIS GUY IN THE CITY, someone my mother-in-law knows, who's got a couple of weird pets: two snakes, a Boa and a Python. He's also got a Pitbull called Mini, which is borderline weird considering that Pitbulls are hated animals these days and to own one is to make a personal statement of sorts, a kind of cranky defiance. The guy's name is Wayne.

Wayne is twenty-four or twenty-five, an unemployed tire changer and not a personal friend of my mother-in-law's but the son of a woman in her Monday night bridge group.

Wayne still lives at home with his mother because his own rented place burned down, something to do with his marijuana-growing heat lamps short circuiting and starting the fire. He's on probation now because of the marijuana business and he's having a tough time getting a job again after the tire place let him go. It was the write-up in the local paper about the fire that did it.

So he's moved back home. He's got a room off the kitchen and he's hung black plastic in the doorway and over the windows because, he says, he doesn't like the light. He's got his two snakes in there with him, in cages. The heat lamps are for them, he says.

Wayne likes to shock the Bridge ladies with his snakes when it's his Mom's turn to host the game; he likes to see them grimace. More often than not, one of the snakes will be draped around his body when he comes out to say hello. No doubt he's operating on some ancient idea of distinction when he shows off like this: he's got rare and exceptional qualities, just like his snakes have, just like rich people had in other times. Wayne's major quality, though, is his intuitive feel for power. Just seeing the looks of horror on the Bridge ladies' faces when he tells them his snakes are really cuddly is enough for him. That and the surprise that guys his own age show when he tells them about his snakes makes Wayne feel that he's a really interesting guy.

The trouble with snakes, though, is that they have to eat

and what they like best is live rats. Wayne's growing them down in the basement. He hasn't bothered to name the rats because they're a crop, after all, and it's not a good idea to get too attached to them. The snakes eat a rat apiece each week. They're brown rats with tiny black eyes and they squeal when they're put in the cages with the snakes.

Mini, the Pitbull, guards the door to the back room where the snakes live. She's particularly fierce when the snakes are having their weekly meal — she'll only let Wayne into the room. He's pretty certain that Mini is strong enough to fight off the snakes should they take a liking to her. So far they've left Mini alone.

Wayne's Mom, Wendy, thinks the whole thing is interesting. "After all," she says, "it could be worse. Wayne could be on drugs, the really hard stuff like heroin or cocaine, or even in jail because you never know with kids these days. At least while he's at home I know he's getting fed."

Rats eat grain. Wendy picks up bags of oatmeal and cracked wheat from the self-serve bins at Save-On Foods. Bulk buying keeps the costs down.

Wayne likes chicken. That's all he'll eat. Ever since his motorcycle accident last summer he's been extra picky about his food. He's a big, beefy guy, pushing two hundred, the youngest of three kids.

Wayne likes his chicken fried or roasted but never cut up in bits and served with vegetables, Chinese style. He likes beer and Mars bars, too, but these he buys with his unemployment cheque. Also motorcycle magazines, which he spends most of the day reading.

The rat crop in the basement makes an awful smell. There are three cages lined up down there, side by side: one for the nursing mothers and their young, one for the teenage rats and a third cage called, appropriately enough, Death Row. It contains the rats which have grown large enough to become dinner. It takes about twelve weeks to grow a full-sized rat.

Even though the smell in the basement is overpowering, Wendy likes to take the Bridge ladies down there and show them the set-up; she's quite proud of her son's ingenuity with the cages. "He might not have finished high school," she tells the women, "but he's sure got a way with assembly line slaughterhouses."

Wendy works as an aide in the behaviour class at an elementary school so her expectations for her own kids are not that high. Wayne's Dad, Frank, moved out last year, just after Wayne moved back. As soon as Frank left, he completely changed his life. Quit his job in insurance and started up a bottle exchange business which isn't doing too badly. He's living with a thirty-five-year-old cocktail waitress named Shirley. They have an apartment in the city. Wayne never visits them. Shirley thinks Wayne's a slob.

Wayne doesn't have a steady girlfriend right now but he's

not worried. His pal Kevin picks him up Friday nights and the two of them tear around all weekend going to bars and any parties they can find.

The weekends are lonely times for Wendy. She won't go into Wayne's room where the snakes are — they make her nervous when he's not there — but she doesn't mind feeding the rats downstairs. It's fascinating, she says, watching the whole procedure. The nursing mothers are never fed to the snakes. She's glad of that. There are two of them regularly spitting out babies. She feels uneasy about the rats on Death Row, though. It helps if she can name them. Her favourite name is Shirley, followed by Frank.

Thank goodness she has her Bridge group on Monday nights to look forward to, she says. Then she can really let her hair down. In recent weeks she's been telling the Bridge ladies that her other son, Bruce, is talking about moving back home. He just broke up with his girlfriend and they're laying off guys at the mill, she tells them, adding that he could get the pink slip any day now. Bruce doesn't have any weird pets, though, just a big Doberman-cross called Jet. Well, why shouldn't he move back home, Wendy asks her friends. The more the merrier.

Recently, my mother-in-law went to another Bridge game at the Snake Pit, as she's come to call it. I'd given her an assignment: to find out the names of Wayne's snakes. She's not pushy about asking questions like I am, so she only overheard some conversation. This is what she heard: one of the snakes is called Melissa. She doesn't know if it's the Boa or the Python but Melissa is four years old and fourteen feet long. She showed me with her hands how wide Melissa's body is — about the circumference of a loaf of French bread.

There's a lady in the Bridge group who won't play when the game's at the Snake Pit, a sub has to be found. She's afraid one of the snakes will get loose and do her in. The Bridge ladies are all nice middle-class women who take pride in their homes. Each one serves something fabulous for tea when it's her turn to have the game — squares, cakes, layered party sandwiches. And they are all fond of Wendy, whose life, they feel, seems to be coming unglued, what with Wayne and the snakes at the house even though she says she loves the company. Wendy's been in the Bridge group for sixteen years, ever since Wayne was Little Wayne. He didn't have any weird pets then.

During that last game at Wendy's house, my mother-in-law saw Bruce, Wayne's older brother. It turns out he'd just moved back home the day before. His dog Jet was being very unpleasant to Mini. Or maybe it was the other way around. There was a lot of growling and barking coming from the kitchen.

Bruce came into the living room to say hello to the ladies. He's thirty. He couldn't shake hands with them, though, because his right hand was covered in bandages. It seems he'd cut off his index finger only last Wednesday with a carving knife while trying to pry apart some frozen hamburger patties for his supper. That's what tipped the scales in favour of his moving back home. The doctors were able to sew his finger back on but Bruce is on some pretty heavy pain pills right now, which makes him want to sleep all the time. And he can't work, of course, maybe for months. He's thinking of trying for Worker's Compensation, telling them the accident happened on the job.

My cousin, who's also named Shirley, has grown-up kids, too. Every time she sees a moving van driving slowly up her street she breaks out in a cold sweat: one of her kids might be paying her a permanent visit. But Wendy doesn't seem to mind about having her kids back home. And she doesn't mind about the weird pets, either.

My mother-in-law says it takes all kinds. She just makes sure that when she's playing Bridge at the Snake Pit she wears her boots and pants and a sweater with tight cuffs. You never can tell what might crawl up a person's body while they're playing cards and not paying attention, she says.

It's because of Wayne's story that I've come to believe that pets, weird and ordinary, should be protected. They're the one thing we have in this nutty world that keep things familiar. They're a constant. Not only that, but they keep the psychiatric profession in check, like cats do with rats. It's scary to think of being overrun with even more therapists and self-help prophets than we already are. Pets are cute, cosmic garbage bins overflowing with human neurosis. They'll listen to your troubles for free and they won't write books or give seminars. By their love and silence they'll help you find your own solutions. Every time.

I hope Wayne's snakes listen to him in that darkened room after the Bridge ladies have packed up their cards and gone home. I hope that when he's feeling miserable he can tell the snakes his troubles. I hope, too, that his snakes sleep with him, that he lifts them lovingly out of their cages and places their scaly bodies in his bed, replacing all the girls he can't seem to keep hold of. But it's sad to think of Wayne at his Mom's house in ten years time, another ageing, perpetual child, or his Mom as an oppressed pensioner.

My mother-in-law says it's a funny old world and not to worry too much about Wendy, you never can tell how things will turn out, hinting that there may be a new man in Wendy's life. She told me that at the last Bridge game, Wendy, a woman known more for her personality than her face, looked beautiful sitting at the card table shuffling the cards and that such unexpected beauty in a person is certain proof of love. I'd never noticed before, my mother-in-law said, but she has those light blue eyes, and she's actually quite handsome for a woman of fifty-five, she hasn't got her foot in the grave yet.

WHAT'S TRUE, DARLING

I suggested to my mother-in-law that maybe Wayne has become Wendy's weird pet because, after all, the definition of a pet fits him: a tamed animal that's treated fondly. And as for the weird part, well…

But my mother-in-law said, "Don't be ridiculous," neatly ending my current weird pet story. At least, I think it's ended. Because last night she started tantalising me with a sequel; she'd heard that Bruce's ex-girlfriend has a pet tarantula called Bocipius. Bocipius? Yes, she said, apparently it has the run of the house.

How do you have a tarantula for a pet? I asked.

Very carefully, my mother-in-law said, very carefully.

Built For Pleasure

WELL, I'M HAVING A BALL. Not saving a cent, but piss on it. Why worry? In March I went to Mexico for a week. Stayed in a condo with this woman Donna; she's an accountant, it's her condo. She said: "It won't cost you a cent, you can stay for free." A week later I was gone. Los Cabos. Met all kinds of Canadians there. One guy from Toronto, a lawyer hiding out from some deal gone wrong, lying on the beach with a couple of girls in bikinis, having the time of his life. I took a pile of pictures.

Couple of days before the trip I went to the track. First race I lost three-fifty. I'm going: I don't believe this. Next race I lost five. That's eight-hundred-and-fifty bucks and only two days before I go to Mexico. And I'm going, what's the matter with you? You've just spent all your Mexico money. But guess what? Day before I leave, I go to the track again. Put thirty-five dollars on a triactor three times and the horses come in. A long shot, twelve hundred dollars. Gave a hundred to the mutual clerk, reached through the wicket and stuck it in her shirt pocket. "Oh," she screamed, "for me!" Then I'm going, I'm outa here. Slapped a couple of hundred on the Visa and took off.

Customs at Mexico couldn't believe it. About my luggage. A carry-on bag, that's all I had. "What you got in there?" they said. "Two pairs of cut-offs, three T-shirts, a toothbrush and a comb, that's it," I said. And walked away from that Mexican airport like nothing could touch me. Everyone else had to wait in the heat and flies for their bags. Not me. I was on that condo balcony drinking rum and pineapple a half hour after landing.

Next month it was Hawaii. For a week. I figured, what the hell? The flights are cheap and I had another place to stay. Another girl from the bar, this one a loans officer in a bank. Sharon. These girls like the company, they're in here all the time. Both of them divorced, living on their own. A couple of nice girls going soft at the edges. "Why don't the three of us get a place together?" Donna's said this more than once. "Be like one big happy family." But living with two women? Get outa here. But they're always fussing over me. Last winter when I had strep? There's Donna at my door with chicken soup. "Figured you must be sick if you're not at the bar," she says. Oh, she knows me. "Randy," she says, "you should be putting some of your money into a pension plan, saving for your old age."

"Yeah, yeah," I go. "Why worry about tomorrow, when you got today sitting on your face?"

Easy come, easy go. That's me. The money I blow. Cashed my paycheque, had nine hundred bucks in my pocket Friday night. Monday morning, there's one-forty left. And I'm going: Where did it go? Then I have to sit down with a piece of paper and think. All right. Three hundred went for what I owed on last month's rent. Another fifty went on groceries. Forty more on wine. Dropped about a hundred in Rossini's on Friday night and another hundred, hundred-fifty at the track on Saturday. (Okay, don't ask: I had forty riding on an exactor in the seventh race and the pair were heading down the stretch when guess what? Second place bumps the front horse and they both get turfed.) Sunday I laid low, watched the game on TV, didn't spend dick, then headed over to Rossini's about eight-thirty for a couple of beers which cost bugger-all. So that's it, five-fifty total. There's over a hundred bucks I can't account for. Jesus, I don't learn.

But these girls, they'd like to teach me. Sharon, she's a laugh. You wouldn't believe the stuff comes out of her mouth. For someone who works in a bank. Had her son living with her for a while, a twenty-something creep doing piss-all, still in bed when she got home from work. Sharon told him: "Get the fuck outa bed ya little shit and get a job." Oh, she's tough. "Randy," she says, "you're a good looking guy, you're not stupid so smarten up and die right." Meaning get serious about her.

"Better not look in this direction," I tell her. "I'm not in the mood for divorce number three."

Two divorces, that's enough. My buddy Morris, he was best man at both my weddings. Is that a laugh or what? Got drunker than skunks both times but not so's you'd notice. And the second wedding to Carol at her sister's place in North Van — that was the best. Everything first class, catered, set up like a restaurant in the living room, with tables and tablecloths and flowers and women serving drinks on trays. I wore a white tux and Morris had a black one done in the same style.

Someone started playing Cat Stevens on the stereo, "Morning Has Broken." But no one had told me it was the wedding march. So there's me, Morris and Frenchie drinking scotch in one of the upstairs bedrooms and Frenchie says: "Uh, Randy, I think you're wanted downstairs." And we come out and there's over a hundred people staring at us and Carol and her father and the minister standing at the fireplace that was made into an altar and the song nearly finished. Boy, Carol was cheesed. But I made it before the song ended. I said to Carol, "Hey, get me to the church on time." And everybody heard and laughed. Oh, it was the best party after that. Frenchie brought a bucket of prawns with him from up the coast and Carol's old man pumped for the champagne. There was a ton of food. We danced halfway through the night. The best party, my own wedding.

It was on our honeymoon, on the flight to L.A. with Carol puking her guts out that we ran into Jimmy Wilson heading down to Santa Anita for the opening. On the same flight. And I'm going, is this fate or what? So sudden change of plans, folks. Say good-bye to Disneyland, folks. Santa Anita, here I come. Made seven hundred the first day, just like that. And lost another fifteen the rest of the week. With Carol sick in the hotel room having the flu, lying in bed watching TV. "Hey," I told her, "order room service, make the best of it, this is Los Angeles, home of the Stars. If you look out the window you might see Arnold Swartzenegger driving by."

After a week, Carol felt better. We had time before our flight home to take a look at Mann's Chinese Theatre. Where the stars put their prints in cement. And you know what? Mel Gibson's hands are the size of a girl's! I put my hand over his runty print and the tips of his fingers come to my middle joints. And you know what they say...big hands, big you-know-what. If I was Mel Gibson I wouldn't go around advertising it.

But home two months and the honeymoon's over. It's like: "Knock, knock, your name Randy? Well, here's another shitload of trouble." Main one being: the market went *pffttt* and I'm stuck with a two-hundred-grand spec house I can't give away. And guys all over town wanting money — drywallers, roofers, bricklayers. One guy, a carpet layer, had his wife sitting outside the house for a whole day crying. "I got kids to feed," she said. I gave her a hundred bucks, that's all I had. Then I'm selling the furniture to pay everyone off. Moved into the spec house to save money but the mortage payment's killing us. I even tore the toilets and bathtubs out of the bathrooms and sold them. Sold the kitchen sink too. And the fridge. Carol was bringing in bugger-all as a bartender.

So pretty soon the bank repossesses, and we're looking at thirty days till we're out on the street. By this time I didn't have a car, I didn't have money, ha! I didn't even have a pot to piss in; I couldn't even walk across the street. So I figure, what the hell? why not take a little vacation, borrow some money from my mother, go someplace warm, Florida maybe, till things blow over. But Carol's going: "I can't take this anymore," and starts dividing up the wedding presents. And it's like: "Here, you take the waffle iron...Oh, no thank you, I'd rather have the placemats..."

WHAT'S TRUE, DARLING

On our first anniversary, Carol's moved in with her mother and I'm drinking Scotch at the hotel with Morris. And I'm going: "Marriage, what marriage? You know anyone around here who's married?"

But I did go to Miami. Not long after Carol split I was working for Hertz, parking the rentals at the airport. I'd only been working there a few weeks when Jimmy Wilson calls me up, says, "Randy, can you give me a lift to the airport, I'm heading down to Miami, to Hylea for the ponies." So I give him a ride in a Hertz Ford, and he says, "Randy, you're the best handicapper I know, why don't you come with me, I'll pay the shot; you handicap for me and I'll give you a percentage of the take." So I parked the Ford in the Hertz lot while he ran into the airport to get my ticket. Oh, it was a beautiful hot day in May; I had nothing with me but what I was wearing, a pair of jeans and a T-shirt, my wallet, a comb, and seven bucks in my pocket. We had to run for the plane, it'd started to take off; they had to open the door, push up the stairs, to let us on. And we're laughing like idiots. The stewardess says, "You guys are sure having a good time," and we order drinks and Jimmy Wilson says to her, "Better bring the second and third round while you're at it, sweetheart, we're in the mood for a celebration."

I phoned Hertz later that night from the Miami Hilton and said, "Uh, I won't be in to work tomorrow guys, the car's in the airport lot."

We were gone three months. Went through over a hundred grand, won and lost. Jimmy had to sell the convertible he'd bought down there for the airfare home and I wrote a bum cheque for the hotel. I was thirty pounds heavier than when I started out and ten shades darker, kept getting mistaken for a Mexican. People here couldn't believe it, that I'd drop everything and go. "Believe it," I said. "Life's too short to sweat it." Everyone I knew got a postcard, even Carol. Sent them care of my mother because I didn't know any addresses. She had a laugh reading them all.

But things over here are great; there's plenty of work, things are booming. I should have moved here years ago. Should have got out of that hole sooner than I did. When they shut down the thoroughbreds at Sandown, I slammed the door on Sidney for good. It was the push I needed. I said, "That's it, toodle-loo, cheery-bye, I'll send you a postcard."

Now I'm framing houses for a guy out Pitt Meadows. Get home from work, have a glass of wine and a bunch of Triskets and that's supper. Sit for a while, have another glass of wine and some cheese then head over to Rossini's. I run a tab. End of the month, if I don't have the cash — no problem, I do some work for the owner. Last month I put in a new countertop in the kitchen. Before that, fixed the stairs out back. It's a great place. Always full of people. Thursdays, Fridays and Saturdays they got live music, piano players, singers. Last Easter they had gospel singers dressed up like a choir. They brought the house down.

But people can't figure it out. Sharon says, "Randy, how do you do it? You never look any older, you don't have any grey hair, you don't even have a gut." Oh, these girls can't stand it. They're always on diets, worrying about their hips and the lines on their faces. I don't worry about any of that. I do what I like. That's my secret. I just have a good time.

And you know what else? My old girlfriend from Kansas has been calling. Divorced now, got two kids, one grown and a fourteen-year-old daughter. First time she called was in April. "When you coming down?" she says.

"Don't know," I says, "I'm going to Hawaii in a couple of days."

"You asshole," she says, "why don't you fly down and visit me?"

"Maybe," I says, "last month I was in Mexico."

"You fucking asshole," she says. Oh, she's a riot. "Have you changed?" she says.

"No way," I says, "I'll never change, I'm fifty, still thinking I'm twenty-five."

"You got that right," she says. "I've never known a guy like you — built for pleasure is what you are."

That's what she said: "Built for pleasure."

That's me.

The Party

THE PARTY'S OVER BUT I DON'T WANT IT TO END. I've barricaded the door with the couch and hat stand, spread-eagled my body against the hallway entrance. Desperate, desperate because it's too early for the guests to leave. Their coats are hidden. I called a cab. Their coats are piled on the back seat of a cab bound for Duncan B.C. Deliver the coats to the Chamber of Commerce, I told the driver, or give the coats to the needy. I told him: If you can't find any needy in Duncan B.C., or if the needy in Duncan B.C. don't want the coats, then take them to Nanaimo or Port Alberni. If necessary, take the ferry to Vancouver; it's my treat. No expense is too great to keep the guests at the party. Yes, clothe the needy. The streets of Vancouver are awash with people going coatless and hatless. It's winter and everyone's needing a decent coat. There's a navy-blue topcoat in a cashmere blend. Several Gortex jackets, wonderful for keeping the rain off shivering bodies. And my guests won't be needing their coats. Not when they'll be staying at my party having the time of their lives. Saying things like: This is the best party; how do you do it? We're so grateful you invited us; it must be a charming life to have such charming parties; and the food and music, you certainly know how to make a splash. There are many fine coats and hats amongst my guests' effects. Did I mention the fake fur cape? The selection of Eddie Bauer toques? The watchcaps? The red felt fedora? Such fine heads for these fine hats to sit upon! With smart haircuts and every one of them blown dry. But they mustn't leave. Not yet. Don't let the guests leave! My mission in life. I've suddenly found it! Keep the guests at the party at all costs! None of this brooding, solitary nonsense. None of these couples with their cold and cranky conversations driving off into the dull night. No, what my guests need is converting to the festive cause. They don't think I've noticed the eye contact over the canapes, the slight nodding of heads between couples, the pause in the party talk, the chatter, the birdsong in the kitchen going suddenly mute, the whispers between themselves, the ill-concealed yawns. Meaning: Time to head out, thanks so much for the party but we really have to go, I'm not feeling well, she's not feeling well, nobody here is well, but your party was delightful, the food so thoughtfully placed about the room, the peanuts, the veggie platter, and the music just so, what was that arresting music anyway, acid jazz? Never heard it before, an acquired taste, we're sure, like oysters or olives, but so interesting and we must get together soon. Grabbing purses, delivering wine glasses to the sideboard. So polite! But there's this groundswell of guests gathering themselves to leave. When the first ones make for the door there's no stopping the flood of guests swarming off my stage. But I won't allow it, will I? I'll stop them in their tracks. I won't allow this false joviality, these preparations to leave. Leaving. Leaving my party. I threw a party. Everyone came, then left too soon. It's barely dark out. This is an outrage. An insult. Why did they even come in the first place if they planned to leave so soon? But won't they be shocked when they can't find their coats? When they find the windows boarded up. There's my husband Martin on the ladder with a sheet of plywood, hammering window after window. Well done, darling, soon enough we'll be turning up the music, dishing out the chili. There's hours and hours of fun left yet. What's the matter with you people? Forgotten how to have fun? What does it take? More booze? More dope? A three-piece band positioned by the fireplace? Was the guest list not to your liking? Listen, when I have a party I expect you to stay a week, have a bath, sleep on the living room floor. I expect you to dance and dance your silly feet off. Turn up the music, Martin, let the guests have the time of their lives. Why else have a party? Think of history. In medieval times, guests were better trained. A party lasted days. Even the Catholic church had parties. Unbelievable as it is, the church once had 197 official feast days. Now if that isn't a party organ, what is? Even in the last century, our very own Canadian farmers in the prairie heartland bundled children and dogs into the wagons heading for a central farm, staying a week, sometimes two, getting drunk and dancing to that old-timey fiddle music. You must have seen the movies of simple farmer folk kicking up their heels. Like that. Or think of Hemingway's Spain, *The Sun Also Rises*. Think of carnivals in South America. You can't have a carnival over a polite sip of wine and one or two crackers, then a rush out the door. A carnival takes longer than an hour and a half — it takes a lifetime. Even our own idle rich, during the early part of this century, went in for long parties, several days at least, covering every shade and nuance of party life. They had cocktails before dinner and dressed up in tuxedos and taffeta, earrings and pearls. Then they played cards and danced to the gramophone, drank port, went for strolls in the garden. They changed their clothes several times a day. Went off to their guest beds, and not always with their own partner. Next day, it was a full breakfast and horse riding or tennis or swimming then lunch then a nap then more cocktails and another outfit and another dinner. And it went on like this for days. We've copied everything else from the early rich but why haven't we copied their parties? I'll tell you why — it's because we're constipated. Our celebrations are squeezed out; they're dry, hard things. And they're that way because you don't know how to be a guest. You thought you'd arrive late and leave early. You thought you'd make an appearance then slip away, unnoticed. You thought you'd leave my party too soon. Well, we've sent off your coats, we've boarded up the doors and windows — you won't get away so easily. Even if we have to tie you up, make you listen to a selection of our music, even if we have to imprison you, goddamnit, you're going to have a good time. You're going to kick off your shoes and dance on the living room rug; you're going to have talks in the wee hours, philosophical talks that will deepen your lives. But I can see you don't agree. You're objecting to the gun, to my husband's use of force, you don't like being herded back into the living room, made to sit on the couches and kitchen chairs. One of you has shouted *terrorists*. One of you has screamed *hostage*, trying to crawl off and dial 911. All of you wanting rescue. Imagine! Wanting rescue from this celebration of life! Do as you're told and nobody will get hurt. You know how these things go; you've watched enough hostage dramas on TV. Just stay calm, keep your heads down, don't make eye contact with each other, don't upset the one with the gun. Martin, my poor darling, he's doing all this for me. He didn't even want a party. What, Carol-Ann, he said, another party? But I convinced him. Look, I said, we'll give it one last try — maybe it's been the menu, maybe the lighting. He didn't expect things to get out of hand but he was prepared — the plywood, the nails, and now the nylon rope and the gun. Well, what did you expect? Don't you understand we're saving you from your own joyless lives? Think of this as a deprogramming session. A few days with us and you'll definitely know what the festive experience is all about. And really, all I required was that you stay longer at my party. Like the song says — "Stay just a little bit longer." Your babysitters wouldn't have minded, what's an extra hour? They'd be grateful for the pay. And what harm would there have been, what's an hour or two of lost sleep if the evening is worth it? But, oh no, you couldn't stick it. You had to make your excuses. Midnight! I would have been content with midnight! But it's only nine-fifteen. Never mind, there's plenty of time now. Days and days. So let's get started. On the count of three, I want everyone laughing. I want mirth on your faces. You can still laugh with your hands and feet bound, with your mouths taped shut. That shouldn't trouble you. So start laughing. That's good. The animated nodding of heads. Also good. I appreciate your getting into the spirit of things. Louder. Now keep that up. I'm just going into the kitchen. Martin will watch you. I'm going to sit alone at the kitchen table listening to your joyful laughing. A pause before the party games begin. Sipping my wine in contentment. Listening to the fabulous party going on behind the kitchen door.

Family Baggage

1. MAKEOVER

May Day weekend. Your older sister visits. And her husband who says, at sixty-four, he's through being an architect, it's a rat race — from now on he's taking acting lessons, he's going to be an actor. He shows us his promo picture, a large, smiling head shot he says he hates, but he also says, what the hell, it's got me a few commercial jobs. Your sister, your mother and I are sitting outside in the sun and your sister's telling me about a new hair product from Clairol that hides the grey because, let's face it, she says, I've got enough grey to warrant a major operation. She says she'll personally escort me to Shoppers Drug Mart to pick out the colour that matches my own. Not only that, she'll supervise the makeover back home. Never one to refuse a gift, I agree, but nervously. Thinking of last night when she gave me a lipstick, one she'd bought for herself but was the wrong shade for her skin. I wore it to dinner, for drinks and snacks at the only bar in the city that carried NTN, the National Trivia Network game, the game they said we'd love, they play it all the time at the Keg in Calgary. The new lipstick turned bright orange and I noticed two or three men (all right, they were old) looking at me in *that way* in the bar, but later in bed you said, I hate that lipstick, it makes you look like a cadaver, so maybe the older men were looking at me more in solidarity than in lust. But now as we're sitting together on the lawn, your sister's husband joins us. He's got one of my books in his hand and he's just read the piece about Gertrude Stein and Alice Toklas, and he says, I don't understand, you talk about Alice being the wife, was Stein a man? And I say, no, no, they're famous lesbians, but of course they couldn't be obvious in the '20s, '30s and '40s. At which point your mother, hearing the word lesbian, perks up and says, That woman? I sat beside her on the plane from Toronto last year and I don't care what anybody says, she's a wreck, her hair and clothes are terrible; if there's anybody who needs a makeover it's Gertrude Stein. And we look at your mother for several long moments before your sister says kindly, Oh, yes? Then I remember it was Gloria Steinem your mother sat beside, but the conversation's moved on to acting in the movies and my book has been tossed on the lawn. Because your sister's husband is lathering his bare legs with suntan oil and telling us anxiously, I've got to get a tan, the last thing I'm going to be is an old man with chicken legs — you see them all the time, scrawny white legs sticking out of horrible nylon shorts; no one's going to give you a part in a movie if you look like that.

2. BONDING

You said the best part of the Vancouver trip wasn't the reading I gave on the fourth floor of a condemned building, in a room that contained nothing but a dozen black chairs and a table-top scattered with leaflets about the Revolution. It wasn't the paid-for hotel room with the window fifty yards from the on-ramp to the Granville Street Bridge, or the dinner in the Japanese restaurant with the poet and her girlfriend, and the girlfriend buying dinner. It wasn't even driving in the city traffic, and the way you suddenly became urban, honking the horn and yelling at pedestrians. And it wasn't leaving the kids and your mother at home with frozen pizza and lukewarm threats, or having a few extra bucks in your pocket to buy chocolate yoghurt on the ferry, beer and chicken wings in the hotel bar. No, what made the trip for you happened after the reading, walking into the first bar in Kitsilano and telling the waiter you were looking for a guy called Doug, and the waiter saying, he's over there with the two girls. It was the way we walked up and tapped Doug on the shoulder and how he turned around laughing, delighted to see you. It was the way he said, *Jesus Christ you asshole*, just like it was twenty, twenty-five years ago when you had that apartment together on Fourth Avenue and both of you bartended in Gastown. Forget drums and that wild man stuff, you once told me; male bonding is when you get pissed with a friend, have a few laughs, puke your guts out, shit your pants, then do it again the next night.

3. RACE CAR

Christmas. A small dinner downstairs with your mother. Someone's given her a set of battery operated lights that she can wear to read in bed, strapped to either side of her head like headlights. After dinner you darken the room, put these lights on your head and pretend you're a race car, making race-car sounds with your voice: *Vroom Vroom*. You're so good at it, you look and sound like a car. We laugh and laugh. Laugh till it hurts. The kids, they'd be five and eight, stand by your side staring. Your brother falls off his chair, holding his sides. He hasn't dressed up for Christmas; he's wearing his old blue sweater, his cords with a tear at the knee. His own kids are with their mother, his ex-girlfriend, miles away. Stop it, you're killing me, he tells you. But you keep up the performance: *Vroom Vroom*. Around curves, bending your body right or left, accelerating, slowing down, spluttering then revving up, a kind of music, a free-form jazz. You speed up hills, slow down in traffic, then roar towards the open road. Besides your headlights, there's only the Christmas candles burning, and the tiny white lights covering the dried branch your mother uses as a Christmas tree, the branch she painted white and brought with her when she moved from Toronto. Happy with the party, she opens another bottle of wine and, filling our half-empty glasses, says: This is like the time your father and some fellas were playing with Chatty Cathy in the back yard and they had the doll in the middle of a circle, a bunch of them drinking and betting on what the doll would say next, taking turns pulling the cord on her back. We laughed that time, too, she said, and I remember that of all the things Chatty Cathy said, the line that came up the most was: I'm wet. Please change me.

4. PICTURE

You take my picture. A full roll of film is used, thirty-six exposures. Black-and-white pictures taken against a white paper backdrop you've attached to the kitchen cupboards because, you say, this is where the afternoon light is the best. Head shots, body shots, shots taken from a ladder, shots taken while crouched on the floor. Your subject wearing black in some pictures, white in others; hair hanging loose or tied back; wearing make-up, earrings, scarves, a turtle neck sweater, a baggy white shirt. And you serious with the light metre, intent, pausing only to drink the red wine you said would keep things relaxed. A Hungarian wine, *St. Stephen's Crown*, a bargain at $6.95. There's music playing, *Slim Harpo Live*, then Clarence Gatemouth Brown. The kids off somewhere; it's a Sunday afternoon, a bright day, whitecaps in the bay. That's good, you say about a certain pose of my head, a shoulder angle, a look. Two glasses of wine and the roll's taken; right away you develop the film. Which one will we choose? A while later you show me the contact sheet and I scream. Because I don't recognise the woman in the pictures: the hair's too thin, the smiling mouth too wide, the face lined, unlovely. The camera never lies, you tell me, your face a study in grimness. You say it again. I'm sick of hearing this, it does lie; it lies all the time, or else you lie, I say. What I don't say is that injured thought

WHAT'S TRUE, DARLING

comes from a radio program I've recently heard. An interview on CBC with a certain poet and the four poems he read: one about wisteria, one about a cougar in a tree, one about a spawning salmon, and one about his lover in her bath. There's something lovely about a woman in her bath, the poet says, and as we all know, my lover is very, very beautiful. I'm going to have a bath, I tell you, and what you say is: we can shoot another roll of film, maybe in the early evening, the light is kinder then. And I say, sure, why not? Give me kindness. But sometime later, after the heat of the bath water has subsided, you're kneeling at the side of the tub and lathering soap on your hands. Slowly, intently, you're washing my legs, arms, back and breasts. Then rinsing my body with the bath water you've cupped in your hands.

M.A.C. Farrant is an award-winning writer and regular contributor to literary magazines. Her first book *Sick Pigeon* (Thistledown) was shortlisted for the Ethel Wilson Prize for fiction and the Commonwealth Writer's Prize, and *Raw Material* (Arsenal Pulp) was shortlisted for the VanCity Women's Book Prize. M.A.C. Farrant lives in Sidney, British Columbia.

BRIGHT LIGHTS FROM POLESTAR

Polestar Book Publishers takes pride in creating books that enrich our understanding of the world and introduce discriminating readers to exciting writers. These independent voices illuminate our history, stretch the imagination and engage our sympathies.

FICTION

Comfort Zones by PAMELA DONOGHUE
"Donoghue establishes herself as a masterful observer of humanity...she is bursting with knowledge about the shades of dark and light in human hearts."
— *Vancouver Sun*
1-896095-24-0 • $16.95 CAN / $13.95 USA

Broken Windows by PATRICIA NOLAN
"When I think of successful literary portrayals of devastated lives, I think of Raymond Carver, Dorothy Allison...After reading *Broken Windows*, I will also think of Patricia Nolan" — *Quill & Quire*
1-896095-20-8 • $16.95 CAN / $14.95 USA

Crazy Sorrow by SUSAN BOWES
"...an astonishingly vivid portrait of small-town childhood. Everyday scenes are so detailed that anyone with an ounce of Maritime history will wax nostalgic."
— *Vancouver Sun*
1-896095-19-4 • $16.95 CAN / $14.95 USA

Rapid Transits and Other Stories by HOLLEY RUBINSKY
"[These stories] will return to haunt the reader in the middle of the night. Forceful and beautifully evocative...these finely crafted stories grab the reader about the throat." — Sandra Birdsell
0-919591-56-6 • $12.95 CAN / $10.95 USA

POETRY

Time Capsule by PAT LOWTHER
Acclaimed poet Pat Lowther died tragically; her husband was convicted of her murder. *Time Capsule* consists of excerpts from a manuscript Lowther had prepared for publication at the time of her death. An important collection by a strong and passionate poet.
1-896095-25-9 • $24.95 CAN / $19.95 USA

Love Medicine and One Song by GREGORY SCOFIELD
"[Scofield's] lyricism is stunning; gets within the skin. Be careful. These songs are so beautiful they are dangerous." — Joy Harjo
1-896095-27-5 • $16.95 CAN / $13.95 USA

Whylah Falls by GEORGE ELLIOTT CLARKE
Clarke writes from the heart of Nova Scotia's Black community. Winner of the Archibald Lampman Award for poetry.
0-919591-57-4 • $14.95 CAN / $12.95 USA

Polestar titles are available from your local bookseller. For a copy of our catalogue with a complete list of our books, contact:
POLESTAR BOOK PUBLISHERS, publicity office
103 - 1014 Homer Street
Vancouver, British Columbia
Canada   V6B 2W9
polestar@direct.ca
http://mypage.direct.ca/p/polestar